## He said...

"I tried meeting women everywhere that #$%! book said, from night school to the produce section at the supermarket. And the only one I even *liked* was Maddie "I'm a Serious Journalist" Hatfield, who is totally *not* what I'm looking for. But ya know, as ornery as she is, I just can't seem to get her out of my head...."

## She said...

"If you meet enough frogs, one of 'em *has* to turn into a handsome prince, right? *Wrong.* All *Finding the Perfect Mate* got me was a whole new batch of frogs. Oh well, at least my very imperfect partner on this #$%! assignment, Derek "Sports Are My Life" Newman, isn't doing any better. Now if I could just stop thinking about *him*..."

∂H
Good

*Dear Reader,*

Well, I'll be honest: I didn't know *what* to write about this month. Women grow up hearing about falling for "the boy next door," but apparently I've always lived in the wrong neighborhoods. And I've never turned to a dating book for advice, preferring to meet men via serendipity. Of course, most recently that's meant being "courted" (and I use the term loosely) by the hot-dog vendor near the train station. (What can I tell you? New York is a funny place.) So I think I'll skip the personal-experience stories this month and get right to the books. After all, they're what you *really* want to know about.

First up, our DADDY KNOWS LAST cross-line continuity series continues with Carolyn Zane's *How To Hook a Husband (and a Baby)*. Here's where that hunky bachelor neighbor makes his appearance. And I'll tell you, if this book were set in a real town, I'd be packing my bags right now, because this man more-or-less next door is a winner.

Then there's Samantha Carter's *Dateless in Dallas*. She hooks up two as-opposite-as-they-can-get reporters to research the advice in the year's hot dating book, and the results are explosive. Of course, they're not what anyone expected, either, but does that really matter when true love is in the air?

Have fun—and see you next month, when we'll be bringing you two more terrific Yours Truly titles, the books about unexpectedly meeting, dating…and marrying Mr. Right.

*Leslie Wainger*

Leslie Wainger
Senior Editor and Editorial Coordinator

Please address questions and book requests to:
Silhouette Reader Service
U.S.: 3010 Walden Ave., P.O. Box 1325, Buffalo, NY 14269
Canadian: P.O. Box 609, Fort Erie, Ont. L2A 5X3

# SAMANTHA CARTER

*Dateless In Dallas*

Published by Silhouette Books
**America's Publisher of Contemporary Romance**

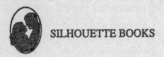

SILHOUETTE BOOKS

ISBN 0-373-52030-1

DATELESS IN DALLAS

Dear Reader,

I've been writing ever since I was a child, when I scribbled the stories I made up in my head into a notebook. It became a dream of mine to one day have a novel published, to go into a bookstore and see my book on the shelf. My dream took a more specific form when I was older and my mother shared her Silhouette romances with me. Then I wanted to write stories about love, to make readers laugh and cry with me. I began dreaming of one day having a novel like that published by Silhouette. With this book, I have fulfilled that dream. I can hardly wait to see it in the bookstore.

I was excited to hear about Silhouette's Yours Truly line, because these were the kinds of stories I most enjoyed reading and writing: fun, contemporary stories about people finding love where they least expect it. As a writer and avid reader, I especially like the twist of having the written word play such an integral role in the story. I've often said that when I finally find Mr. Right, it's bound to have something to do with words in print, as much time as I spend buried in words—whether books, newspapers, magazines, letters or e-mail.

*Dateless in Dallas* was probably the most fun I've ever had writing a book. This book is especially for anyone who's ever searched the world for something special, only to find it closer to home than they ever would have guessed. I hope you enjoy reading it as much as I enjoyed writing it.

With warmest regards,

Samantha Carter

To my mother, who introduced me to romance novels,
then told me she was sure I could write one.
And to the members of Dallas Area Romance Authors,
whose guidance turned a naive, young aspiring writer
into an author.

# 1

*Tired of being alone? There is a way to find that special person for you. Hundreds of happy couples have tried these successful methods to find each other. This guide will tell you where to find all the top-notch singles—just like yourself in Dallas.*

Madeline Hatfield chuckled as she skimmed the back-cover copy of *Finding the Perfect Mate*, the book she found waiting for her in her desk chair. Her co-workers gave her no end of grief about her lack of a love life. This insipid little book had to be their latest trick. She flipped the book over to see a note stuck to the front. The note said, "See me about this. Rhona."

So now she knew who the culprit was. Rhona Correy was Maddy's boss, the features, entertainment and life-style editor of the *Dallas Journal*—and self-proclaimed life-style coordinator for Maddy. Clutching the book, Maddy dropped her knapsack on her desk and stalked over to Rhona's office.

"Is this supposed to be some kind of a hint?" she asked as she stepped through the door.

Rhona looked up from her computer and whipped off her rhinestone-studded cat's-eye glasses. "Of course not,

Maddy darling. You know I never make judgments about a person's life-style. It's an assignment.''

"*Finding the Perfect Mate* is an assignment?'' Maddy asked, planting herself in the chair beside Rhona's desk and crossing her arms over her chest. This ought to be interesting, she thought.

"This book is all the rage. Everyone's talking about it. It flies off the bookstore shelves,'' Rhona said as she leaned back in her chair and laced her fingers behind her head. "In fact, I wish I'd written one like it myself. I could retire soon. But what everyone wants to know is, does it really work? I want you to find out.''

"Find out? You mean find couples who used the book to find each other?''

Rhona shook her head and grinned. Maddy had seen that grin before, the time she'd been assigned to try to sneak backstage at a rock concert just so she could write about the experience of being a groupie. She had almost gotten herself arrested, even if she did walk away with a coveted autograph. Rhona had a talent for devising offbeat assignments. "That would be boring,'' the editor said. "I want you to test the advice yourself and see if you find Mr. Right.''

"Now, Rhona, you are beginning to tamper here. You want me to find someone, don't you.''

"I didn't say you had to settle down with him if you do find him. I just want to see if you can find him using this book. And I want you to write about your experiences along the way.''

Maddy's eyebrows shot up. "You want me to share my dating life with the city of Dallas?''

"It's not your real dating life. It's work. In fact, we'll run the columns anonymously.''

"I don't know about this one, Rhona," Maddy hedged. "I can see it already, in giant headlines across the front page of the life-style section, Madeline Hatfield Can't Get A Date To Save Her Life. Reporter Attracts Weirdos And Jerks."

"Don't sell yourself short, sweetheart. The only reason you haven't found someone is because you've been looking in the wrong places. With some help from this—" she indicated the book Maddy held "—you might look in the right places. Besides, you won't be in this alone. I want to get a male perspective on this, too. We'll assign one of the men from our staff to do the same thing."

"Which man?"

"That's up to you. Since I'm making you do this, I'll at least give you a choice there. Pick someone, and I'll take care of it with management. You'll both still have to carry out your normal duties, of course, but turn in expense reports from any of your dates. We'll take care of that for you. I look forward to seeing your first column. Today's Wednesday. Do you think you could have something for Monday morning's paper?"

Which meant she wanted something to happen this weekend. Maddy had already planned on a relaxing Friday night curled up with a good mystery novel and a bowl of popcorn, but it looked like she would have to change her plans. "Yeah, I guess I can have something for you, but there are no guarantees I'll have anything worth reporting."

"You'll come through for me, I know you will. And by the way, Maddy," the editor added with a careless wave, "I have a couple more assignments for you on your desk. The usual, you know, weddings, new restaurants, a press kit for a new band. Work your magic for me." Before Maddy had made it out of the chair and through the door, Rhona was already back at her computer, her cat's-eye glasses firmly in place on her nose.

Magic was what it took to make her usual assignments interesting, Maddy thought as she made her way back to her desk in the cramped newsroom. As a small, upstart newspaper, the *Journal* didn't have the budget or the reputation to do elaborate stories or get any big-celebrity interviews. It also didn't have the budget to pay top salaries, so Maddy's monthly budget required a little prestidigitation, as well. Still, she wouldn't trade her job for anything, except perhaps a posting as correspondent in some international hot spot. But that wouldn't happen while she was working for the *Dallas Journal*, so she enjoyed her position as the paper's only feature writer.

At her desk, she coaxed her computer terminal to life and went to work. She wrote nearly a dozen wedding stories for the Sunday paper, adding her own unique flair so they were at least slightly more interesting than the fill-in-the-blank stories found in most newspapers. She perused the press kit and made an interview appointment with the band's publicist, whom she suspected was a friend studying public relations in college. Then it was time for lunch.

When she looked up from her desk, the usually bustling newsroom was almost deserted. It was Wednesday, so that meant Don Graham would be off covering the city council meeting. A couple of other reporters might be getting neighborhood reaction to whatever the city council was up to this time. When she considered that the other reporters she knew were out on assignment, it accounted for most of the paper's small staff. Everyone else must have gone to lunch without her. It looked like she was on her own.

She planted her black velvet bowler hat firmly on her head, slung her knapsack over her shoulder and started to head for the door before turning back to pick up the book.

She might as well get a head start on Rhona's latest hare-brained assignment.

Maddy ate her salad mechanically as she studied the book. It seemed to her to be a compilation of the kind of advice usually found in women's magazines, or else the kind of advice her mother offered when she began to despair of ever becoming a grandmother. The only remarkable thing about the book was that it was selling so well. There must be a lot of lonely people out there.

"Well, if it isn't the Mad Hatter," a booming voice cut into her concentration, and she looked up...and up...and up to see the speaker.

"Why, Derek," she said sweetly when she recognized the newspaper's sports writer. "What brings you downtown to slum with those of us who aren't in the sports world?"

Derek Newman put down his tray, eased his muscular, six-foot-four frame into the seat across from Maddy and smiled the grin that had made co-eds at the University of Texas go weak in the knees. "And how are things going in Eastern Europe, madam foreign correspondent?" he replied, reminding Maddy why his smile had never made her swoon.

"Oh, they're still fighting. I'm covering the situation from a safe distance." She tried to disguise how much his casual jibe stung. The only time she was dissatisfied with her life was when she was reminded of what she had wanted to do ever since she'd been in college. Back then, when she and Derek had worked on the campus newspaper together, she had never let him forget that he was just a jock who wrote, while she was going to be a serious reporter, a foreign correspondent. Now he returned the favor by constantly reminding her of her earlier, more lofty goals.

*"Finding the Perfect Mate,"* he read off the cover of her book between bites of his half-pound hamburger. "Finally doing something about your social life, I see."

"You're one to talk. You didn't even have a date for the Christmas party last year."

"Neither did you," he reminded her.

"Well, this isn't for me. This is work. Rhona wants me to test the advice and see if it really works."

"Good idea. If it works for you, everyone should find it helpful. There will be weddings all over Dallas."

Maddy tried to think of a stinging retort, then came up with a better idea. She studied the man across the table from her. He was a basic athletic stud, straight out of every cheerleader's fantasy—wavy blond hair, blue eyes, great body. But he hadn't played football since his junior year in college when a knee injury cut his career short, and he could at least read and write. He also was basically a nice guy, when he wasn't talking to Maddy. It was a miracle he was still single. But he might not be for long if she had anything to do with it.

Fighting back the wicked grin that threatened to tug at the corners of her mouth, she asked, "How are things going out at Valley Ranch this time of year? I imagine it's a little slow since the Cowboys are in the off season."

"Yeah, it's a little slow," he admitted. "Just the usual stories about how the players are spending their off-season, coaching changes, rumors, that sort of thing. Why?"

She glanced down at the table and ran her finger up the side of her glass, leaving a trail through the condensation. "Well, I'm supposed to get a male perspective on this assignment about finding a mate in Dallas. Rhona said I could choose anyone, and she'd work it out with management." She looked him straight in the eye and allowed herself a satisfied smirk. "I think I'll choose you. I'd like to see what kind of luck you have."

Derek nearly choked on a bite of his burger, coughed, then took a hasty swig of his cold drink. "Me?" he croaked. "I don't need help finding a mate."

"I didn't say you did, even though I don't recall ever seeing you with anyone or even hearing about you seeing someone. I just said I'd like to see how this works for you. And you're probably less busy right now than any other man on the staff."

"You expect me to go out on the Dallas meat market and sell myself, then write about it?"

"I have to do it. Why shouldn't you? What's wrong, Derek, is the big, strong jock afraid of a few helpless little females?"

He snorted. "Helpless, my foot, especially if they're anything like you. And no, I'm not afraid. I just have better things to do with my time."

"Like what?" Maddy asked, with a curiosity that went beyond her interest in the issue currently under discussion. She had long wondered what the typical Adonis did in his spare time without managing to make it into any of the city's social columns.

Derek took a long time to chew and swallow the bite of hamburger he had just taken. "You know—stuff," he said with a casual shrug that contradicted his reddening face. "I work out some—you don't think it's easy keeping a body in this shape, do you?" he asked with a broad grin. Maddy rolled her eyes as he continued. "I keep up with the literature, *Sports Illustrated, Dallas Cowboys Weekly,* that sort of thing. I watch game tapes. And I have that radio show, remember? I keep plenty busy."

"It sounds like you need a social life even more than I do. You're in this with me, Newman, whether you like it or not. I'm turning your name in to Rhona this afternoon."

This time, Derek was the one to give her an evil smile. "If I'm going to have to do this, we might as well make it interesting. What do you say to a little side wager?"

Maddy shook her head in disgust. "I swear, do you men have to turn everything into some sort of competition? All those sports must warp the brain."

"It would definitely make things more interesting for us, and that would make it more fun for our readers, even if they didn't know about our little contest. Be honest, Maddy, were you even remotely intending to try very hard on this assignment?"

She stiffened. "I always work to the best of my ability."

He shook his head. "That wasn't what I meant. I have no doubt your columns would be fascinating and well written. But would you really have tried to find someone, or would you just have gone through the motions?"

She had to think about that one. To be perfectly honest with herself, she had no intention or expectation of finding a real relationship through this assignment. "Okay, so you're right about that one," she said with a sigh.

"I thought so. And how interesting would a bunch of columns saying, 'I Struck Out Again,' be for our readers? But, if we had some incentive to really try, it could be the kind of thing to sell papers."

"Very persuasive, Newman, but what kind of bet did you have in mind, and how do you propose to determine a winner? Is it whoever scores first?"

"Actually, I was thinking of something a little more meaningful than that, more like who develops a lasting relationship."

She shook her head. "No, that won't do. We'd have to wait for the first break-up to declare a winner."

"Okay, how about the first person to have three dates with the same person, and it has to be someone you genuinely like, not just someone you're going out with to win the contest."

Maddy's eyebrows shot up. "Derek!" she exclaimed. "That's as good as saying it's whoever scores first."

"Huh? You lost me there," he said, his forehead creasing in confusion.

"I thought that was a universal guy thing, that you expect to sleep with someone on the third date."

He flushed from his neckline to his hairline. *How cute, he's bashful,* Maddy noted. "That—that wasn't what I meant," he stammered. "I just meant that if you've gone out with someone three times, you're moving in the direction of actually having a relationship instead of just dating. And it means you are more than a little attracted to that person."

She nodded. "Okay, three dates it is. And it can't just be to win the bet. In fact, you forfeit your prize if you dump the person within two weeks of winning."

"Agreed." Then he waggled his eyebrows and leered at her. "Of course, if you insist, sleeping with someone automatically wins. But you have to be brave enough to tell, and you have to produce some kind of evidence."

"Three dates, and you have to produce some kind of evidence of the date," Maddy said firmly. "What you choose to do on those dates is up to you."

"Sounds good to me. Now, what should the prize be? Loser washes the winner's car?"

She shook her head. "No good. My car would fall apart if you washed away the dirt that's holding it together. And let's make it more interesting than that."

"How about the loser is the winner's loyal slave for a week, at the winner's beck and call."

"What kind of slave?"

"Get your mind out of the gutter, Maddy. I meant someone to wash dishes, do laundry, run errands, cook, chauffeur and generally take care of all the tedious details of life."

"I can agree to that. I'll have to start thinking of ways to keep you busy."

"Don't count your chickens," he warned. "I may be rusty, but remember, I was once the terror of Austin."

"Yeah, if you're lucky, your reputation won't have followed you to Dallas."

"I think I'll start letting my laundry pile up so you'll have plenty to do."

"Before either of us starts making plans for what we'll do when we win the bet, we'd better start making plans for our assignment," Maddy reminded him.

"Okay, what's the first thing we're supposed to try?" Derek asked.

Maddy picked up the book and flipped to the first chapter.

# 2

#### ⟶⟵

*It may seem obvious, but one of the best places to meet members of the opposite sex is at a nightclub. Almost everyone will be there in hopes of meeting someone, so you're sure to find someone who might be interested in a relationship. You're also more likely to find active, outgoing people.*

*Pick a place that specializes in the type of music you like, and you're more likely to meet someone who has something in common with you. Once you're there, get out on the dance floor. People are attracted to people who seem to be having fun. On the other hand, if you're not feeling very outgoing, try sitting quietly and reading a book or writing a letter. That's sure to generate interest and is a good way to start a conversation.*

Derek double-checked the apartment number scribbled on the back of the envelope, then knocked on the door. He found it hard to believe Maddy Hatfield lived in a place like this. If she had been his daughter, sister, distant relative or even an insignificant other, he wouldn't have stood for her living alone in this neighborhood. Then again, it was near the hospital and medical school, so if something did happen to her, she would have plenty of help nearby. From the looks of things, most of her neighbors were starving medical students.

Maddy was hooking an ethnic-looking beaded earring to her earlobe as she answered the door. Derek didn't know whether to stare at her or at her apartment. Its interior was almost as shabby as its exterior. He caught a glimpse of cluttered bookcases built from cinder blocks and boards, theater and art exhibit posters thumbtacked to the walls and a worn futon that had seen better days.

He turned his attention to Maddy herself. He was accustomed to her usual eclectic style of dress, but he wasn't accustomed to her looking like this. She wore some kind of black leotard that covered her like a second skin from her shoulders to her ankles. The scooped neck of the leotard revealed a hint of the curves of her breasts. A gauzy skirt in an Asian print did nothing to conceal her slender, shapely legs. A black velvet beret perched on top of her sleek chestnut pageboy. She looked devastatingly sexy, and even though the object of the outing was supposedly for both of them to meet someone, he wasn't sure he wanted to turn her over to anyone else.

"Wow!" he managed to gasp when he remembered to breathe again. "You look great, but I'm not sure I'm dressed appropriately," he said, eyeing his jeans and starched oxford-cloth shirt. "I wasn't sure how you dress for Deep Ellum." He wondered again how she had managed to talk him into going to Dallas's trendy, funky nightlife district.

"You'll be fine," she assured him. "People come to Deep Ellum from all over Dallas. People will just think you're a preppy drone."

"Gee, thanks. That gives me a lot of hope for my prospects this evening. But remember, tomorrow night you're going country dancing with me."

"Whatever you say, Romeo. Let me get my purse and we'll go." She disappeared for a moment, then reappeared with a tiny bag on a long string. She stepped outside the apartment, shut the door and locked it behind her, then tucked the key in her bag and slung the long string around her neck.

"We'd better take my car," she said as they walked down the sidewalk to the street.

"What's wrong? Embarrassed to be seen in a pickup truck?"

"Not at all. It's just that my car is too junky to steal or trash, and parking is at a premium. My Volkswagen can squeeze into places a truck can't."

"If you insist," he said, giving her a gallant bow. He almost changed his mind when he saw her car. It was a Volkswagen Bug, probably older than either of them. It belonged in a museum, not on city streets, but it wasn't in museum condition. "Are you sure this thing will get us there and back?" he asked doubtfully as he studied the battered old car.

"Of course," she replied, unlocking the door. "You might want to shove the seat back a bit."

He also might want to sit in the back seat and let his legs stretch into the front seat, he thought as he squeezed himself into the car. He wasn't claustrophobic, but it was a tight fit by himself. When Maddy slipped into the driver's seat, he was almost overwhelmed. It didn't help that she was wearing a clingy outfit that covered most of her body while hiding nothing. He rolled down the window so he could get some fresh air. He doubted the Bug had air-conditioning.

Maddy handled the stick shift like a pro as she drove into downtown, toward Deep Ellum. Derek had a feeling she avoided the expressways because the car probably wouldn't make it up to highway speed. The engine noise was loud enough at thirty-five miles per hour to make any attempt at conversation futile.

She finally parked the Bug in what appeared to be a makeshift parking lot. As they left the lot, she handed several bills to a man seated in a lawn chair at the lot's entrance. "Come on," she said with a tug at Derek's arm. "We've still got a bit of a walk ahead of us."

The crowd, mostly dressed in variations of basic black, was much larger than Derek had expected on a Thursday night. "It's not even the weekend yet," he commented.

"But it's almost the weekend. A lot of people begin celebrating early."

"From the looks of some of these people, the celebration never ends," he commented, noticing the amazing variety of body parts one could pierce and decorate with jewelry.

"Don't be judgmental, Derek. Just think, Miss Right could be here for you."

"Somehow I doubt it." He didn't find tattoos attractive, and he preferred hair colors that could possibly have come from nature, but he refrained from saying so to Maddy.

Maddy came to a stop at the doorway to what looked like an old warehouse building. Derek pulled her back with a hand on her elbow. "Wait a second, there's not even a sign here. How do you know this is a legitimate club?"

"It's only been open a short time, but trust me, this is *the* place to be. I reviewed it a few weeks ago. When they stop having to turn people away, maybe they'll get a sign."

"Then how are we going to get in?"

"I gave them a very favorable review." As if to verify her words, the doorman waved them through with a smile. "I've also been back a few times since then."

"Wait just one second," he said, planting his heels firmly into the floor. "If you've been here before without meeting Mr. Wonderful, why are we bothering?"

"I thought I'd give you a head start. Besides, I wasn't looking at the time. I was just out with friends." She grabbed his arm and dragged him deeper into what seemed like a black pit filled with throbbing music. Maddy's head, shoulders and hips were already moving with the beat.

"Let's dance!" she shouted above the noise.

He shook his head. "I think I'll watch awhile. Just to get a feel for the place."

She shrugged. "Suit yourself." Then the crowd on the dance floor swallowed her.

Once his eyes became accustomed to the darkness and the flashing lights, Derek found an empty table where he could sit with his back to the wall and watch the dance floor. He had gone to clubs on Sixth Street in Austin a few times when he was in college, but this place was beyond anything he had ever experienced. He felt like a country bumpkin visiting the big city for the first time. Oh, well, he thought, Friday night it would be his turn.

A waitress came by, and he ordered a beer for himself and a wine cooler for Maddy. He wasn't sure what she drank, but he thought that might be a safe bet. When the drinks came, he sat sipping his beer and watching the crowd on the dance floor.

None of the women he saw even remotely appealed to him. He preferred the fresh, wholesome type who might be capable of carrying on a decent conversation. Most of the women he saw looked like creations of makeup, hair dye and spandex. His gaze kept returning to Maddy. She didn't look at all out of place here, yet she retained the same fresh, appealing quality she always had.

But still, there was something different about her tonight. Her body moved sinuously, seductively, with the beat of the music, and her eyes were half-closed as though she were lost in a world of her own. The music changed, and Derek looked away for fear she'd catch him staring at her. Developing an attraction to his partner was not on the agenda for this assignment, and he knew it wouldn't be well received.

Maddy left the dance floor, her eyes darting around until she saw him, then she threaded her way through the crowd to his table. "Whew!" she gasped, wiping sweat off her forehead with one arm as she picked up the wine cooler with the other and took a large swig. "Thanks!" Her forehead wasn't the only part of her sweating. The exposed skin of her chest glistened, and the occasional droplet disappeared between her breasts.

"Found anyone interesting yet?" he shouted, forcing himself to look at her face rather than the rest of her.

She shook her head and leaned forward to shout in his ear. "It looks like the SMU kids have invaded us tonight. They're all babies. And the men who are here don't seem to be interested. I'm doing everything I know to flirt on the dance floor, but no one seems to have joined in." She took another drink, then said, "Care to join me this time?"

He shook his head. "This looks a bit too strenuous for my bad knee. I think I'll try the other suggestion of sitting quietly."

She nodded and danced her way back to the floor. Derek watched her until she was once again part of the throng of dancers, then he took a small memo pad and a pen out of his shirt pocket and jotted down ideas for the column he would have to write about this experience.

A tap on his shoulder jolted him out of his concentration. He looked up to see a curvaceous blonde leaning over him. So that odd piece of advice about sitting in a corner reading or writing had some merit to it, after all, he thought. The woman said something to him, but he couldn't make it out over the roar of the music.

"I'm sorry, I missed that," he shouted back to her. "What did you say?"

She leaned closer and yelled in his ear, "I said, what'cha writing?"

He shrugged. "Just some observations. Nothing interesting, really."

"Huh?"

He tried again, shouting louder. "Nothing much."

She nodded and shouted something else with a jerk of her head toward the dance floor. This time he didn't have to ask what she had said. "No, thanks!" he shouted. He emphasized it with a shake of his head so she wouldn't have to ask him to repeat himself. She shrugged, fluttered her fingers at him and moved on to the next man.

So much for that, he thought. Even if he did manage to catch someone's interest by sitting quietly and writing in a trendy dance club, it was too loud to carry on enough of a conversation to get to know someone. He jotted the idea in his notebook.

"Don't tell me you're already working on your column. You don't even have anything to report yet." This time the voice shouting into his ear was familiar, and he was able to make out the words. He looked up to see Maddy standing over him, breathing hard and sweating.

"Oh, but I've already struck out," he said.

She pulled up a chair and sat beside him. "You, too, huh? I'm beginning to feel like a grandmother out there. I asked someone what he did, and he said he was majoring in business. I could have kissed the kid who asked me what *I* was majoring in.''

"Shall we cut our losses and leave?"

"I'm with you, Romeo."

Derek's ears were still ringing as he and Maddy walked down the street to what passed for a parking lot. He was surprised to find that her car was still there. But then, no self-respecting car thief would be caught dead driving that Bug.

"Was that a total waste, or what?" she asked as she started the engine.

"It was your idea," he reminded her, shouting above the engine noise. He was afraid his ears would never be the same after this night.

"Yeah, well, we'll see how well things go tomorrow night at your honky-tonk."

"At least at my 'honky-tonk,' as you so quaintly put it, people actually dance together. They aren't just part of a mob of writhing bodies."

"Don't knock the mob of writhing bodies until you've tried it, cowboy."

Her teasing statement conjured up a vivid mental image, and he deliberately changed the subject before his mind took it any further. "Is the Mad Hatter's collection extensive enough to include a cowboy hat?"

"Of course. I live in Texas, don't I?" She shot him a mischievous sidelong grin. "But just to embarrass you, I may decide to find something incredibly funky that would be so out of place in your honky-tonk that every eye in the place would be on me."

"Nothing the Mad Hatter does would surprise me."

She was going to surprise him if it killed her. Maddy stared at the collection of hats that had earned her nickname and tried to decide which one to wear. She didn't want to look too conventional, but she didn't want to look weird, either. She wore skin-tight black jeans, black high-heeled cowboy boots with silver tips on the pointed toes and a white lace bodysuit that was discreetly lined in pale pink. To go with it, she was torn between a black felt cowboy hat and a white satin baseball cap. A knock at the door forced her to make a snap decision she was sure would surprise him: she'd go bareheaded for a change.

When she opened the door, Derek's reaction told her she'd made the right decision. His eyes were just about bugging out of his head. "See, I'm really not bald," she said.

"Huh? Oh, yeah, you're not wearing a hat, are you." Then he regained his composure, smiled and shook his head. "You look great. I have a feeling you'll make quite a stir tonight."

She was torn between frustration and delight. He hadn't even noticed that she wasn't wearing a hat, but he had said she looked good. He didn't look so bad, himself. He wore snug, neatly pressed Wrangler's, a starched white western shirt and low-heeled cowboy boots. "And you don't look like you're auditioning for a country music video."

He raised an eyebrow. "Is that supposed to be a compliment?"

"Yes. I hate it when men wear those splashy, obnoxious cowboy shirts."

He shook his head and grinned. "Then you're not going to find too many men who appeal to you tonight."

"I already knew that. Let's get this over with."

This time, she let him drive. His truck would be more appropriate tonight. Her old Bug would have been the only one of its kind on the lot, and they'd probably have been laughed out of the joint for arriving in it.

The honky-tonk was housed in what looked like a former department store in an old strip shopping center. The
parking lot was filled with pickup trucks, many of them with
gun racks in the rear windows. A cluster of men wearing
hats that had to be at least thirteen-gallon size stood near the
entrance. They all wore western shirts so bright Maddy was
sure they required batteries. "We might as well not even
bother going in here," she muttered to Derek. "Men in hot
pink shirts are a real turnoff for me."

"We're not here just for you," he reminded her. "And
aren't you being a bit superficial?"

"Don't get on your high horse," she snapped back, then
asked, "By the way, do they have a mechanical bull in
here?"

"*Urban Cowboy* was more than a decade ago. There's
just dancing, drinking, pool and pinball in here."

"Ooh, sounds like fun. Let's go." Maddy allowed sar-
casm to color her words, but she had to admit that he'd been
a pretty good sport the night before.

Derek circled the parking lot, found an empty space and
stopped the truck, then killed the engine. He was out and
around to Maddy's side of the truck before she had her seat
belt unfastened. With the courtly manners of a traditional
southern gentleman, he opened her door for her and helped
her down from the truck cab. Maddy didn't know quite how
to react to this. She could barely remember the last time a
man had actually helped her out of a vehicle. Her more
feminist instincts urged her to take affront, but she decided
to enjoy it.

A blast of country music as loud as anything played at any
Deep Ellum nightclub greeted them as they entered. As
Derek paid the cover charge, Maddy studied the joint's interior. It was even more vast on the inside than it looked
from the outside. A huge dance floor filled the middle of the

cavernous space. At one end of the dance floor was a stage, on which played the band responsible for the racket assailing Maddy's ears. A mirrored ball overhead scattered flecks of light over the dancers, who spun and twirled around the floor with intricate moves that looked as well-choreographed as any music video.

The other three sides of the dance floor were surrounded by tiers of seats and tables, with the top tier reserved for pool tables and pinball machines. Cowgirls and cowboys hung on the rails overlooking the dance floor. A pall of smoke hung over the whole scene.

Derek gave up trying to get receipts for the cover charge and took Maddy by the elbow to lead her to a table. A pair of girls wearing painted-on jeans and halter tops passed them. *And I thought my jeans were tight,* Maddy thought as she tried not to stare. As Derek and Maddy took their seats, the music changed and the crowd on the dance floor, moving as one, fell into a dance routine that made Maddy think of a Nashville aerobics class.

"This is definitely going to be pointless," she declared. "I'll look like a fool out there. I won't know what I'm doing."

"It's just a line dance," Derek reassured her.

It looked more like herd mentality to Maddy, who was more accustomed to dances where even partners didn't do the same thing. "How do they know how to just start doing that particular dance?"

He smiled sheepishly and shrugged. "To be perfectly honest, I have no idea. I don't come here often enough to know any of the group things. I can just handle a basic two-step."

"I don't know even that much." She sighed.

"Don't worry. The next time they play a nice slow song I'll teach you."

The tempo of the music changed, and as if on cue, the herd on the dance floor dissolved once more into couples. Derek took Maddy's hand and said, "Come on, let's go. We can practice a bit in a quiet corner."

As if there was such a thing in this place, she thought. He found a niche out of the way of the flow of waitresses and patrons, then stopped and put his right arm around her, with his hand resting just below her shoulder blade. "Okay, now, put your left arm on top of my arm and just rest your hand on my shoulder," he instructed her. She followed his directions, and he took her right hand in his left.

"Now, listen to the beat of the music. The basic rhythm for this dance is quick-quick, slow-slow. It's sort of a shuffle followed by a couple of steps." He loosened his hold on her and demonstrated. "You just do the same thing backward."

"And if I'm going backward, how will I know where I'm going?"

"That's my job. I guide you."

Maddy wrinkled her nose. "I'm not so sure I like the idea of this." What a throwback to the Neanderthal era, letting the man lead the way.

"Don't worry, it's pretty easy," he said, misinterpreting her comment. "Even a drunk cowboy can do it."

She shrugged and said, "Here goes nothing." Stepping back into Derek's arms, she waited for him to find the beat of the music and begin moving forward. When he did, she attempted to move her feet to match his. The results made her grateful for the metal toes on her cowboy boots. Their feet kept getting tangled up, so that her feet were either under his or on top of his.

"This is pointless," she finally said, sagging against him.

"You're almost there," he reassured her with a gentle squeeze on her shoulder, which pressed her even closer to him.

*So, this is what a body like his feels like up against you,* she thought absently, suddenly realizing why all her friends seemed to go for the hunky type. She could get used to this.

But not with Derek. Remembering her assignment, she took a step back to increase the distance between them. "Man, it's hot in here," she said, wiping sweat off her forehead with the back of her hand.

"Yeah, the ventilation leaves something to be desired. You can come here in January without a coat." He raised an eyebrow at her. "Are you game to try again?"

"Oh, why not." This time, she pretty much got the hang of it after they circled their little corner once.

"See, that's not so bad. Let's try it on the floor," Derek encouraged her.

She reluctantly let him lead her to the dance floor. As they waited at the edge of the floor to find a break in the flow of dancers, she felt like she was about to merge onto an expressway. This time, she was glad Derek was "driving" as she employed her emergency fallback method for merging into heavy traffic: she took a deep breath, closed her eyes and went for it.

When she opened her eyes, they were in the middle of the swarm of dancers. One couple whirled by, turning with every step. "Don't even think about trying that," she warned Derek.

After one turn around the dance floor, she relaxed somewhat and allowed herself to look around at the other dancers. Some seemed even less experienced than she was, but a few looked like dancers from a country version of a Broadway show. A few of the men were rather attractive, but most of them were firmly attached to bosomy blondes. She didn't see anyone she would be interested in pursuing seriously.

The song ended before they completed their second turn around the dance floor. "Do you want to try another one, or do you want to sit down?" Derek asked.

She was still weighing her answer, deciding just how masochistic she was feeling tonight, when she felt a hand on her elbow. She turned to see an earnest young cowboy wearing a starched shirt in a red-and-black flame pattern.

"Excuse me, but would you like to dance the next one?" he asked.

This was an even more difficult decision. He seemed perfectly nice, and he was even kind of cute, but then she noticed the telltale bulge in his lower lip. He might not be chewing tobacco at the moment, but she could tell he did regularly. Texan or not, that was one habit she found truly revolting. Suppressing a shudder, she said, "Sorry. New boots. They're killing me." He nodded and touched his hat in farewell as he moved on to the next woman.

She turned to see Derek watching, his eyes twinkling in amusement. "I take it you want to sit down," he said. She nodded, and he led her back to their seats. "What was wrong with him?" he finally asked. "He seemed perfectly nice."

"Yeah, and you try kissing someone with a mouth full of tobacco."

"No one said you had to kiss him."

"Still—" she let her voice trail off as she shuddered again "—that's just something I can't overlook."

He surveyed the crowd and turned back to her. "If you could pick out anyone in here to spend more time with, who would it be?"

She chewed her lower lip as she studied the men in the room. The first answer that came to her mind was *you*, but she cut the word off before she said it out loud. She didn't want to give him ideas, just because he was up against some pretty sorry competition. "No one here really strikes my fancy. What about you?"

He raised an eyebrow and smirked. "I'd be pretty nervous about trying to pick up women here. Try it on the wrong guy's girl and you could get your lights punched out. And it seems to be a real date night tonight. I might have better luck on a ladies' night."

"Does that mean we can go home?"

"If you want to."

She stood up. "We've got some columns to write."

*Hers:*

It seems like conventional wisdom that a nightclub would be a good place to meet someone. If people didn't believe this, these places would go out of business. But I had never before visited one for the sole purpose of meeting a man.

This may be a case of never finding something you're actually looking for; I certainly had dismal luck this time around. Even at my favorite place. When I started looking at men as something more than dance partners, all of a sudden none of them met my standards. I don't know whether this was just a particularly off crowd, or if during all those other times I've gone just to dance I never worried about whether a man was younger than I am, not a great dresser or not a good conversationalist, as long as he could dance.

And I had even less luck at a place outside my normal realm of activity. So I would say that one bit of the book's advice was correct. *Stick with places you enjoy.*

My advice on using nightclubs as a place to meet men is *don't*. But if you want to go out and have a good time, and if meeting someone interesting would be a fortunate coincidence but not your goal, then go out and have a blast.

*His:*

Whether or not you have any success meeting dating prospects in a nightclub is a factor of your personality. If you aren't comfortable asking strangers to dance or dancing with strangers, you might as well stay home. This kind of meeting ground requires an outgoing, confident person.

I would have to agree with the advice on choosing a place that fits your taste. I tried going someplace new, and while I had my cultural horizons expanded, I wouldn't have wanted to spend time with anyone I met there.

I also tried the alternative advice about sitting quietly in a dance club, reading or writing. While this did attract attention, it was impossible to carry on any kind of conversation with the loud music in the background. Try this in a more mellow jazz club, but don't bother in a louder setting.

My visit to a place more in keeping with my normal musical tastes made me realize just how shallow your judgments about people have to be in this kind of setting. You can find someone attractive, but you have no way of knowing if there's anything beyond looks, and you have no way of knowing who you might be missing, because she didn't happen to catch your eye in the crowd.

# 3

---

*Don't underestimate the value of everyday activities for meeting someone interesting. They provide a nonthreatening environment in which people are relaxed enough to be themselves, and since everyone has to shop and do laundry, there will be plenty of people to meet.*

*Try visiting a grocery store on Friday or Saturday night. Women—take note: this is when many single men do their shopping, and you can generally bet that if they're in a grocery store on a Saturday night, they're available. Early evenings on weekdays are a good time for meeting professional men and women who pick up groceries on their way home from work.*

*A grocery store in an upscale neighborhood is a good choice, but avoid suburban areas without apartment complexes. You'll just find families there. Look for a store with a coffee bar or deli and a nice selection of imported or gourmet foods.*

Maddy put the book down and glanced at her watch. It was almost five. She could try the grocery store thing this evening. It was already Thursday night, and she needed to have a column for the Monday paper. The first columns, printed earlier in the week, had been a hit. People had even called and written the paper to express an interest in the subject. She just hoped she had something to report this time.

She dropped the book in her knapsack and got up from her desk. "Knocking off early, Maddy?" Don Graham asked from the desk next to hers. His face showed the strain of an impending deadline and an unwritten story. He was probably jealous.

"Nope. I'm going on assignment," she replied over her shoulder as she headed out the door. And it was work, despite what the other reporters seemed to think. She pulled out of the newspaper's parking lot just before the evening rush began and aimed her Bug north of downtown, avoiding the freeways. The big gourmet store on her way home should be a good target. She rarely shopped there because her budget didn't allow for upscale groceries, but she could afford a splurge this time, and she might be able to count it as a work-related expense.

Her little Volkswagen looked out of place in the store's parking lot. There was a Jaguar parked on one side and a Mercedes on the other. "Well, *my* car's a collector's item," she said to the two luxury cars as she strode to the store entrance. She paused before entering to straighten the floppy brim of her velvet hat, then took a deep breath and approached the automatic door, which swung open to welcome her.

It wasn't a particularly huge store, but it was the first grocery store she had ever seen with a second-floor balcony overlooking the produce section and bakery. She took a hand basket and headed toward the fruit section. Her eyes widened at the prices, but she was accustomed to shopping at the farmer's market on Saturday morning. In addition to the usual staples, there was a wide variety of more exotic produce. She raised her eyebrows at the prickly pear fruit. Who would want to eat that? And pay *that* for it?

She paused by a selection of produce she couldn't identify and picked up a large, creamy-colored bulbous thing. According to the label above the shelf, it was a jicama. What was a jicama, and what did one do with it, she wondered.

"Just what exactly is a jicama, and how do you eat it?" said a voice beside her. She kept herself from jumping in shock at hearing her own thoughts repeated out loud. This could be a good sign. She turned to see a dark-haired man standing next to her, studying the exotic produce with a perplexed air.

"I was just wondering the same thing myself," she admitted.

"Oh," he said, sounding somewhat disappointed. "I was kind of hoping you would know, since you picked one up. May I?" he asked, reaching for the jicama she held. She handed it over to him, noting as she did so the absence of a gold band on his left hand. So, he could be a prospect.

As he turned the jicama over in his hands, she took the opportunity to study him. He was kind of cute, not a head-turning knockout, but fairly attractive in a classic, preppy kind of way. His dark brown hair was neatly cut and combed, and the eyes behind the wire-rimmed glasses were an attractive shade of blue. He was of average height and average build, and he wore a navy suit with white shirt and red tie. He wasn't exactly what she was looking for in a lifemate, but he could make a decent date.

He finally shrugged and put the jicama back in the bin. "I think I'll stick to potatoes, lettuce, tomatoes, apples and carrots," he said.

"Every so often, I get wild, daring and exotic and buy a papaya," she said with a smile. This wasn't the most scintillating of conversations, but it was a start.

He smiled in response and moved on to the apple display, where he stared at the selection in dismay and said, "Do they not have just plain old apples anymore?" She looked at the display to see that each variety of apples was labeled with a fancy name and an even fancier price. To her, a Granny Smith apple was getting fancy. She took it as a good sign that he seemed to feel the same way. A true yuppie would have known just which variety of apple would most impress his friends.

"I think the regular red apples are at the end of the aisle," she told him. "And in the next row they have oranges that don't have their own passport."

He smiled at her, began selecting apples and promptly seemed to forget she was there. She hovered around the produce for a few minutes more. To justify her lingering, she picked up a stalk of broccoli and put it in her basket. It was on sale, and was actually a pretty good buy. When he still hadn't said anything more to her, she decided to move on to the rest of the store.

She bypassed the dairy case—there were only young mothers there. At the back of the store, she found the seafood counter. A lobster tank stood in front of the counter. She peered into the water to see the lobsters, looking suspiciously like insects, crawling along the bottom of the tank. Was this a pet store, or a grocery store?

"Do you ever get the urge to take one home and keep it in the bathtub?" said a voice beside her. He was back.

"I was just thinking they look too much like scorpions," she said, fighting back the silly smile that threatened to overwhelm her face. "I don't know if I'll ever be able to eat lobster again."

"I'd rather not become acquainted with my food before I eat it," he agreed. He then smiled sheepishly and said, "If we're going to keep running into each other like this, we might as well introduce ourselves. I'm Tim Morris." He held out a hand to her.

She shook it and said, "I'm Madeline Hatfield, but everyone calls me Maddy." This was even better than she'd hoped. She had come here planning to try to pick someone up, and here she was being picked up. She couldn't wait to tell Derek.

"Are you here looking for anything in particular?" he asked.

"No, I'm just Zen shopping. I wander through the store and pick up whatever interests me." That sounded much better than admitting she was there looking for men.

"Do you think the bakery or deli might interest you?"

"Bakery, yes. Deli, no."

"Okay. Mind if I join you in the bakery?"

"I wouldn't mind a bit." As she walked with Tim through the store, Maddy found herself wondering what to do next. She felt a bit like the dog who, after a lifetime chasing cars, finally caught one and didn't know what to do with it.

"Do you shop here often?" Tim asked.

"Not really," she replied, grateful that he had taken over the conversation. "Usually I go to the farmer's market or to a little neighborhood store, but I was on my way home from work, so I stopped by."

"Where do you work?"

Maddy paused before answering, afraid she might give too much away. He'd probably drop her instantly if he knew he was about to be the subject of a newspaper column. "Downtown," she hedged.

"Really? So do I."

Before the conversation could get any more awkward or shallow, they reached the bakery section. Since she had said that was why she was here, she knew she had to find something. She perused the bread selection, finally picking up a round loaf of wheat bread. "Well, that looks like all I need for dinner," she said.

He looked at the loaf of bread and stalk of broccoli in her basket and raised an eyebrow, but he didn't comment. "Well, then, it was nice meeting you, Maddy" was all he said. She started to head toward the cash register with the sinking feeling that she had struck out, after all, but her hopes lifted when he called her back.

"I know this is going to sound really stupid," he said. "And I want you to know I'm not in the habit of shopping for women at the supermarket, but would you like to have dinner Saturday night?"

Maddy blinked. There might be a spark of truth in that silly book. She never would have believed that this, of all suggestions, would work. Then the nagging voice in the back of her head, which she was sure her mother had planted, warned her about going out with strange men. She shoved it aside, as she usually did. He didn't seem the ax-murdering type. "Yeah, I'd like that," she said.

He smiled, which made him look even cuter. "Great. Why don't we meet somewhere? How about the Starlight Grill?" It was a casual place nearby, and certainly a safe place to meet a stranger.

"Sounds good to me."

"Shall we meet at seven, then?"

"Okay, Saturday at seven. I'll see you there." She couldn't wait to go home and call Derek. Unless he had been really busy, she was the first to actually get a date.

\* \* \*

*Any time you get out of the house, you're increasing your chances of meeting someone new. That includes not only grocery shopping, but also trips to the post office, the dry cleaners and the gas station.*

*You can also get some exercise in the process. Walking, in-line skating or bicycling, especially in singles-oriented neighborhoods, is a good way to see other people also concerned about keeping in shape. (In other words, great bodies!) This isn't a quick meet-and-greet tactic. It may take time to become familiar with fellow joggers who follow a similar schedule. Start with a smile and a nod when you pass, then later work up to a greeting, and eventually you may be running together.*

*If you want a quick meet-and-greet, though, try walking a dog. Women are drawn to cute, friendly dogs, while men will be impressed with big dogs. If you've seen the Disney movie* 101 Dalmatians *you may know how a properly rambunctious dog can do some matchmaking of his own, if he has a long enough leash!*

Sadie certainly fell into the cute and friendly category, but Derek was afraid women would be more likely to laugh at him than be impressed as he followed the dachshund down the sidewalk. Her little legs were moving as fast as they could go, but Derek still felt as if he was barely moving. He wished he had followed his better judgment and just gone to the grocery store rather than walking the only dog he could find to borrow.

Still, he was getting attention. Everyone he passed turned to look at the mismatched pair. A few attractive female joggers paused and smiled as Sadie yapped up at them, but then they went on their way without noticing Derek. He didn't mind all that much. They gave him the impression they put more effort into improving their bodies than they did on improving their minds.

He passed a lawn where a toddler played while her parents worked in the flower beds. The little girl saw Sadie and squealed with delight. "Doggy!" she cried out as she toddled to the sidewalk. Derek stopped and allowed her to pat Sadie on the head. The little dog's tail was wagging so hard it looked like it was unbalancing her hindquarters.

Derek watched the little girl and the dog play and smiled. As the book had promised, he was picking up women. The book hadn't specified what age they would be. If he was really lucky, some fabulous knockout would jog by, see how good he was with children and be really impressed.

But he wasn't lucky. No one slowed down long enough to notice him. "Come on, Sadie," he said to his charge when the toddler tired of playing with the dog. "I'm taking you home, then I'm going grocery shopping. It worked for Maddy." The gloating message he had found on his answering machine a few nights ago had made him desperate enough to try walking Sadie. He couldn't let Maddy show him up.

"And now I'm talking to a dog. Maybe Maddy's right and I do need a social life." Sadie yapped at a passing car. Derek wasn't sure if that meant she agreed.

Maddy crawled out of her Volkswagen, hoping Tim wasn't watching her. There was no way to accomplish that maneuver gracefully. Straightening her skirt, she noticed with some surprise that her hands were trembling. The butterflies that took wing in her stomach seconded the motion. "Okay, I admit it, I'm nervous," she muttered softly to herself. "I don't usually do this sort of thing."

She shuddered when she realized exactly what she was doing. She was going to dinner with a man she had met in the produce section of the grocery store. She didn't know anything about him. Already she could hear her mother's objections.

"For all you know, he could be a serial killer who finds his victims where they least expect it," the warning voice inside her head scolded. She decided against telling her mother about this one so she wouldn't have to hear the scolding a second time.

As if she weren't already nervous enough, she had struggled for an hour trying to figure out what to wear. Tim seemed the conservative type, so she had found the most conservative outfit in her wardrobe—a long, skinny black knit skirt, white T-shirt and brocade vest, topped with a velvet cloche hat. He would probably faint when he saw her and pretend not to recognize her, she thought.

Squaring her shoulders and forcing herself to walk toward the restaurant entrance with a confident stride and a bright smile, she hoped the evening didn't end in disaster.

Tim was waiting for her just inside the restaurant's entrance. His outfit was conservative enough to make her look like a cutting-edge fashion plate. He wore khakis and an oxford-cloth shirt, the "casual Friday" uniform of corporate America. Still, he was as cute as she remembered, she noted with relief as he stepped forward to greet her.

"You came!" he said.

"You didn't think I would?"

"Not that," he assured her with a laugh. "I just realized later how crazy this was. I still can't believe I asked out someone just from meeting her in a grocery store."

She laughed, too, some of her nervousness melting away. "Yeah, it is a bit crazy. But it wouldn't be the first time someone said that about me." *That didn't go so badly,* she thought.

The hostess announced their table was ready and Tim ushered Maddy forward, then held her seat for her. *Another good sign,* she thought.

Perusing the menus and selecting food gave them a brief reprieve and a chance to think of new conversational gambits. For once in her life, Maddy wasn't sure what to say next. How did one go about having a conversation with someone one didn't know at all?

*Duh,* she then thought with disgust, fighting back a wry smile. *You're a reporter, dummy. Interview him.*

"What looks good to you?" she asked. *Might as well start with neutral territory,* she told herself.

"I'm wavering between the ribs and the fish."

She noted the bravery of being willing to eat ribs on a first date. She usually tried to avoid anything that was likely to smear all over her face or dribble down her chin. That also eliminated pizza and most pasta dishes.

"I think I'll go for the soup and salad," she said. There was still the risk of getting lettuce stuck between her teeth, but otherwise everything on the menu contained enough fat grams to wipe her out for a week.

"You're not some kind of health food nut, are you?" he asked. "You certainly don't look like you need to lose weight."

She decided to take that as a compliment, however awkward it sounded. "I'm no fanatic, but I'm not big on grease."

His smile faded, and he looked like a puppy that had just noticed a rolled-up newspaper. "Oh. We should have picked a different place," he said.

She fought back the urge to roll her eyes. She liked sensitive men, but this could get annoying if taken too far. "No,

I really like the soup and salad here. That's probably what I would have ordered anywhere else.''

He immediately perked up again, and she could see that it would take some effort on her part to keep his spirits up. The jury remained out as to whether or not he would be worth the effort.

The waitress showed up to take their orders, and once again the feeble conversation lagged even further. This was definitely time for the hard-hitting investigative reporter to step in. Maddy took a deep breath and asked, "So, what do you do, Tim?"

"I'm an accountant. Nothing very interesting, really."

She had to agree with that, but it wouldn't make for much of a conversation if she left it at that. "But there must have been something about it that's interesting for you to choose it as a career," she said.

He shrugged, adjusted his glasses and said, "I guess I've always loved numbers. I find them fascinating."

Thirty seconds later, she regretted asking the question, but she supposed it was too late to interrupt and say, "You're right, accounting is boring."

He started at the beginning—the very beginning—of his fascination with numbers. "I learned to count before I knew my alphabet," he said, then went on to describe how he had counted all the money in his piggy bank every day. He was just getting to the part where he started his first savings account when the waitress brought their food.

Maddy hoped to use the opportunity to begin another conversation since his monologue had been interrupted, but before she could open her mouth, he was continuing. "That savings account really fascinated me. Every night before I went to bed, I would calculate how much interest I had earned."

With a sigh, Maddy gave up and tuned him out, concentrating instead on her meal and pausing occasionally to smile and nod when he seemed to expect it. She hoped Derek was having better luck than she was. Then she groaned inwardly at having to tell Derek how her date had gone. Especially after she had gloated so much about having a date.

After returning the dog to her owners, Derek changed into jeans and a shirt and drove up the road to Valley Ranch's grocery store. It was upscale and it was in a neighborhood with a lot of singles, so it fit the book's parameters. He wasn't sure what he would find there on a Friday night, but he needed something to eat for breakfast the next morning, anyway.

The store wasn't particularly full, not like it was with the after-work crowd. The video section had been picked clean, and there wasn't anything left to rent but a few old, bad dramas. He was sure the video section was a good place to meet singles right after work on a Friday. He wondered if he got extra credit for coming up with his own strategies.

He headed to the dairy section to pick up a gallon of milk, then wandered down the frozen foods aisle. A young woman stood in front of the ice cream freezer, gazing into its depths. She looked like she was preparing for a chocolate rampage. He had bravely gone up against three-hundred-pound monsters in college football, but he didn't have the courage to come between a woman and chocolate.

The coffee sampling station was deserted, but he helped himself to a cup of the store's special blend to fortify himself for the rest of the expedition. The produce section had the best selection of women he had seen all night. Unfortunately, one had a baby in her cart. Another finished choosing oranges and put them in the cart of the man nearby.

The third woman was rather cute and young, with long, curly hair. She was frowning at the grapes, as if she could lower the price or improve the quality with just a glare. He moved in next to her and picked up a bunch of grapes. "I hope they get better this summer," he said by way of an opening remark.

She looked up at him as if noticing his existence for the first time. "What? Huh? Oh, yeah, the grapes," she said. "These are pretty good." She put a bunch in her basket and moved on.

"And he's out," Derek muttered under his breath. At the rate he was going, he might as well find out how Maddy liked her laundry done. He picked up a bag of English muffins and checked out, then went home. He could get a head start on his column, then use Saturday night to continue work on what he referred to as The Great American Novel.

Once again, he kicked himself for even suggesting the bet. Maddy was right, he loved competition, but this assignment was really eating into what little spare time he had.

Forcing himself to be charitable, he hoped her date went well.


This was not going well. Maddy felt her eyes glazing over as she stared across the table at Tim. He was still talking about the joys of accounting, and she had yet to say much of anything. Looking for the bright side, she realized she hadn't yet had the chance to tell him she was a reporter. He might not recognize himself in the column she would write.

But that didn't mean she was having a good time. She had sat through what seemed like hours of discourse on accounts payable and spread-sheet software. Actually, it had only been through dinner and dessert, but if the waitress didn't bring the check soon, Maddy wouldn't be responsible for her actions.

"Enough about work," she finally interrupted. "It's Saturday night! What do you like to do for fun?"

He gazed at her blankly. "Fun? I guess I just watch television and read business magazines."

She sighed. What had given her the idea that she might have anything in common with him? Ah, yes, they both needed to buy food. He had been charming at the store, but his conversational skills didn't go beyond small talk or himself. She couldn't help but think of the old joke: "Enough about me! What do *you* think about me?"

The waitress rescued her by bringing the check. He took it, calculated an exact fifteen percent tip, then left the precise amount of the total bill on the table. Maddy watched in amazement. She would have needed a calculator to figure the bill, but that didn't mean she wanted to hear all about it.

He escorted her out to the parking lot, then paused. She hoped he didn't suggest they do something else. If he did, she had a dozen ready excuses.

Fortunately, he didn't. "It's been fun, Maddy," he said, extending his hand to shake hers. "I'll give you a call sometime."

"Yeah, that would be great," she said, then hurried off to her car before he could remember that he didn't have her phone number. She didn't relax until the restaurant was safely in her rearview mirror and she was sure she wasn't being followed. Not that she was worried he would stalk her and kill her. She was more afraid of having to hear more about accounting. From what she could tell, he had only discussed the first page of his résumé.

Back home, she took off her elegant cloche hat, kicked off her shoes and settled down on her futon. A wicked grin crossed her lips when she thought of how Tim would have viewed her apartment. He was probably a neat freak. Her typical clutter would make him break out in hives.

As disgusting as it was to have to admit it, she'd had much more fun when she went out dancing with Derek, even if she hadn't had much luck in the mate search. At least he could talk about something other than his work, and he let her talk, too. And he was much, much cuter, even if he could be a jerk sometimes.

On impulse, she picked up the telephone, then dug in her purse to find the newspaper staff roster and dialed Derek's number.

He answered on the second ring. "Hey, Newman, it's me," she said.

"Maddy?" His voice had a distant, distracted quality to it. Maybe she was interrupting something.

"Quick question. How'd you do this weekend?"

"Struck out." A wave of relief washed over her. She wasn't interrupting anything. They were still even. And he was still unattached. *What brought that on?* she wondered about the last thought.

"What about you?" he asked.

She sighed. "He was an accountant. And he told me all about it. In detail."

"I'm sorry to hear that."

"No, you aren't. You're just glad I'm not one up on you."

"So you're not going to see him again?"

"Not if I can avoid it, although he might make a good anesthetic if I ever need surgery."

He chuckled. "Well, we can try again next week. What's on the agenda, then?"

She picked up the book from the floor by the futon and flipped through the pages. "Oh, this one should be good.

We're to get involved in a political cause or religious organization.''

"That should at least give us an opportunity for conversation.''

"I hope so. It can't get much worse.''

*Hers:*

I've been shopping in grocery stores most of my life. When I was a kid I got to ride in the cart and was happy when my mother let me pick out my favorite breakfast cereal. If I didn't get cookies, I'd try to get my way by making a scene in the store. When I was in high school, I volunteered to go to the store because all my friends worked there.

But I never knew I'd go to a grocery store with men at the top of my list. In a way, this advice did work, for I found a nice man. We had some witty repartee in the produce section, and by the time we got to the bakery, he was asking me out.

But finding a man in the produce section doesn't narrow the population base much. We all need to eat, and eating was about all this gentleman and I had in common, as we found out when we went out for dinner. That doesn't mean you won't find Mr. Right in the freezer aisle, but I don't think it's very likely.

Shop for food in the grocery store, but don't count on them having a special on men.

*His:*

I must say this about the advice to try walking a dog to attract women—it works. But if you're picky about the age of your women, you might want to try something else.

Sadie, my dog for a day, was a lovely little dachshund, and women did notice her. Unfortunately, the only one who approached me was about two years old, and she had eyes only for Sadie. I might as well not have existed.

Men, forget what the book says about cute, friendly dogs. Find one that fits your image, whether or not it's big and scary. Then you'll still have your self-respect, even if you strike out.

I also tried the grocery store idea. Don't try this on a Friday night and don't get between a woman and her chocolate craving. I might suggest going to the video section right after work, or perhaps early on a Saturday evening. That's where the traffic is. Just stand in front of the section that interests you and ask for suggestions from other patrons. If nothing else works for me, I'll give this a try and tell you how it works.

# 4

— ▶ ◀ —

*Most people want something beyond the merely superficial when they're looking for a mate. They want to have something in common, so that they'll remain interesting to each other for a lifetime. Sometimes you can luck upon someone like this in a social setting, but it's more likely to happen if you make it happen.*

*You can make it happen by doing things you happen to find interesting. You'll then automatically have something in common with the people you meet in those settings.*

*For a relationship that's grounded in common values, you can't beat a political organization or a church group. The people you will meet there are involved in a cause beyond their day-to-day lives.*

This tactic showed much more promise than the others she had tried so far, Maddy thought as she perused the newspaper to see which community groups might be meeting soon. Maybe this time she could have a decent conversation with a man. And even if she didn't find someone interesting, she had been planning to get more involved in the community for a long time. Now she had a reason to find a way to do her part.

"What's on the agenda for our hopeful lovebirds this week?" Maddy jumped when she heard Rhona's voice over her shoulder and hurried to hide the *Dallas Morning News* she was reading. Her editor wouldn't think kindly of her reading the rival newspaper in the middle of the newsroom.

"We're up to the third chapter," Maddy reported. "This week, it's a political or religious group."

Rhona perched on the corner of Maddy's desk and crossed her legs. She wore leopard-print leggings, a switch from her usual all-black wardrobe. "So far, it's going like a charm, isn't it?" she said.

"Well, if you call one date with an accountant a charm, I guess it is."

"I'm not talking about your success, I'm talking about the project's success. People are reading you, darling. Did you hear the morning show on K-Hits this morning? They mentioned your columns between songs all morning long."

Maddy didn't find that too exciting. It meant that more strangers knew about her pathetic attempts at a social life. She might be anonymous now, but eventually her identity would be revealed. Then maybe she should try for a posting in Bosnia or Timbuktu and fulfill that dream of becoming a globe-trotting foreign correspondent.

Rhona patted her on the shoulder. "Keep up the good work, and good luck," she said as she headed back to her office. Then she stopped and turned back around. "Oh, yeah, and that Derek really is a dream, isn't he? I'm amazed he doesn't have women falling all over him."

Derek chose that moment to rush into the newsroom. He almost collided with Rhona, but he appeared to be too distracted to have noticed what she was saying about him. He deftly caught the features editor before she could fall, moved her out of his way, and continued to Maddy's desk.

"Maddy, can I borrow your terminal?" he said without bothering with greetings or small talk. "The power got knocked out in my neighborhood by some construction project, so I can't use my computer. It won't be fixed for another hour and I've got a really hot story to turn in, and I've got to be at the radio station in two hours. Someone's already using the sports department terminal."

Maddy thought about making one of her usual jibes at him for being an unprepared jock, but a look at the strain around his eyes told her now was not the time. She got up from her chair and motioned toward it. "Be my guest," she said. "I'm not on deadline."

He sat down, pulled a folded sheaf of papers from his back pocket and a pair of gold-rimmed glasses from his shirt pocket, put the glasses on, then started typing furiously. Maddy watched him work, her thoughts drifting back to Rhona's earlier comment. He *was* pretty dreamy, especially now, for some odd reason. The glasses made him look less like a jock and somehow more intellectual, although she already knew he was intelligent enough to be able to string together a few words. The lenses only served to magnify his bright blue eyes.

He frowned and chewed on his lower lip as he typed, and Maddy's fingers itched to brush the blond cowlick off his forehead. Why was he still single? she wondered. And how could he have struck out so miserably so far in their project, when even she'd had at least one date? Then she remembered the way he had acted at both the Deep Ellum nightclub and the honky-tonk. Despite his natural self-confidence, Derek was shy. The former football hero who spent a couple of hours a day on the radio chatting with thousands of people about sports was so shy he had a hard time asking anyone out.

Maddy caught herself smiling at the thought. She might as well start making plans for tasks he could do when she won the bet. If she had been looking for the perfect torture for him, she couldn't have done any better. This would get him back for every teasing comment he had ever made to her. But his shyness also made him suddenly more appealing. It added a touch of vulnerability to his otherwise larger-than-life persona.

She was still smiling when he finished typing, saved his story into the system and took off his glasses. "Thanks a million, Maddy," he said as he put his papers and glasses back into their respective pockets. "You saved me on this one. Sometimes, there are drawbacks to working in a remote location."

"Oh, sure, anytime I'm not on deadline," she said, trying to wipe her silly smile off her face. "Have you decided what you're going to be doing for this week's effort?"

"I guess I'll try the church thing. At any rate, it will make my mother happy. I've been trying to find a good church since I've been here. But, I admit I haven't looked very hard, especially during football season when I'm working Sundays. And Mom never lets me forget about it."

She nodded. "Okay, then I'll try the political thing. Actually, I think I'll try to find a group doing something about homelessness."

"Good idea. Just don't let me see you on the evening news being hauled off to jail for an illegal protest," he said with a smile. "Well, I've got to get across town to the radio station. See ya later, Mad Hatter." As he passed her, he paused to flip up the brim of her hat and plant a light kiss on her forehead. "Thanks again," he said over his shoulder as he left the newsroom.

Maddy hoped Rhona hadn't been watching, but there was little chance of that. The woman probably had surveillance cameras everywhere so she could keep the supply of office gossip going. Just in case, Maddy tried to keep her cool and not let her reaction show. With trembling hands, she returned her hat to its proper position and straightened her skirt. She resumed her seat at her computer terminal, but found it hard to concentrate. She reminded herself that the object of her assignment was to meet someone out in the world, not to develop a hopeless crush on a man she'd been immune to for more than five years. It had just been a friendly little kiss, so why was she acting like he'd declared his undying affection for her? With an act of will, she forced herself to focus on her work instead of on the way his blue eyes had seemed to twinkle as he bent closer to kiss her.

Derek slipped into the back of the church, just a few minutes late for Wednesday-night Bible study. This was one of those contemporary, nontraditional churches that met in an office building, and it supposedly had a membership consisting mostly of young, professional singles.

The congregation was still singing hymns, and he didn't recognize the one they were singing. Part of that could be because instead of the traditional organ and piano accompaniment, they were using an electric guitar, drums and synthesizer. This was a big switch from the small-town church he had attended when he was growing up.

As he fumbled through the hymn book, looking for the correct hymn, he glanced over the small congregation. There were several young women, a couple of them sitting by themselves. If he had played this right, he could have sat beside one of them. But this evening he was just there to get a feel for the place and check out its potential, he reminded himself. Sunday morning he could make more of an effort to meet people.

The preacher began the sermon, and Derek let his eyes wander once more. There was an attractive young woman across the aisle two rows in front of him. She probably wouldn't have caught his eye on a busy street, but here he was intrigued, if only because her being here meant she might share some common values with him.

The minister's voice intruded on his consciousness, bringing with it a sense of guilt. He really couldn't compare values with her if she was there because of her beliefs and he was there because he wanted to meet women. It was probably his upbringing and his parents' lectures about not paying attention in church that were coming to the forefront of his mind again after all these years, but he had the paranoid suspicion that God was going to strike him with lightning for his improper motives. If he continued coming to this church and just happened to develop a relationship with someone, then that was fine. But, he vowed to himself, he wouldn't try to ask someone out immediately just so he'd have something to write about. Then he forced his mind back to the sermon.

The service ended and he made his way up the aisle, hoping to avoid having to speak to anyone. He wasn't entirely successful, for a few church members stopped him to welcome him. It was with great relief that he made it to his truck in the parking lot without having to face any of the younger women. If he came back, he wanted to do so with a clear conscience.

And he was sure none of his avoidance tactics had anything to do with the fact that Madeline Hatfield had recently become so much more attractive than he remembered her from college. He couldn't possibly be comparing every woman he saw to her.

But not a single woman in that congregation had been wearing a hat.

Maddy arrived early at the community center, while the room was still being set up for that evening's meeting. She helped unfold a few metal chairs, which gave her the opportunity to meet some of the group's leaders. Unfortunately, they were all married.

She had picked the Homeless Outreach organization out of the newspaper because homelessness was one problem in society that really troubled her. She had no idea what she would do if she were suddenly out on the street without a home, so she couldn't bear the thought of anyone else being in that situation.

Once the room was set up, she took a seat near the middle of the room and watched as people filed in for the organizational meeting. Another reason she had chosen this organization was the fact that it was just getting started. She would have the chance to be in on the beginning. She noticed one or two attractive men, and she knew that if they were at this kind of meeting, they couldn't be shallow, self-centered yuppies.

One of the more attractive men took a seat at the end of her row. He glanced in her direction as he sat, and she gave him a slight smile in return. She crossed her legs and gave him another smile, but he didn't accept her nonverbal invitation to move closer. Oh, well, she thought, maybe she'd have a chance to strike up a conversation after the meeting.

Then the meeting started. The organizers laid out the ground rules, and others then stood to make suggestions for the organization's efforts. Soon, a big debate began over whether to take political action or to focus on local efforts. The man at the end of Maddy's row stood to speak. "We've got soup kitchens and shelters. What we need is to make the government responsible enough to do something," he said. Several others in the group applauded.

Maddy suddenly forgot her original reason for being there as her temper built. As a reporter, she had seen all too often how people loved to shift responsibility to someone else when the power to make a difference was in their own hands. With a glance at the man, she rose and said, "But political grandstanding isn't going to make the situation any better for people who are hungry and out on the street. Sure, we have shelters and soup kitchens. But do we have enough to meet the needs? I'd rather be sure the needs of my fellow citizens are met than march on Washington and make the national news." An even louder round of applause followed her remarks, and as she sat down, she felt a rush of adrenaline. She hadn't done anything like that since college, when she had joined a demonstration on the university's West Mall.

The man at the end of the aisle glared at her, and she remembered why she was there. *There goes that possibility,* she thought. But with his attitude, she was sure that any date with him would have been a repeat of the date with Tim, only with a monologue about his social activism rather than his career in accounting.

The meeting continued, with the group finally agreeing to support one of the local shelters with donations and volunteers, while forming a political committee to bring concerns to the local and state governments. Maddy felt a warm glow of excitement and goodwill when she left the community center. It wasn't until she reached her car that she realized she hadn't made the slightest effort to strike up a conversation with any of the men there, and she was glad. She wondered if she would have received the same round of applause for her speech if everyone there knew that she had come for the sole purpose of meeting men. Probably not, she thought with a shudder.

There was a chance that she might meet someone in the course of doing the volunteer work she had signed up for, but she wasn't going to set out to do so. She felt cheap enough already for having come for such a shallow reason. She wasn't going to compound that mistake.

She wondered if Derek felt the same way about this tactic. As serious as he could be, he probably had shoved the thought out of his mind as soon as he entered the church. At least she hoped so. She didn't want him beating her at their game. Knowing her luck, he'd meet some wonderful woman who would make the perfect, traditional wife for him, and together they'd have beautiful blond, blue-eyed babies. She told herself that it wasn't jealousy to think this way. She just didn't want to have to clean house for him for a week.

When she got home, the light on her answering machine was blinking. She hit the Play button and heard Derek's voice. He sounded dejected. "Maddy, it's Derek. I might as well concede this whole game to you. I don't care if this is supposed to be guaranteed advice, I can't go to church to pick up women. If this is what it takes to have a relationship, I give up."

She smiled to herself as she picked up the phone. She had memorized his number, and now punched it in on the keypad. He answered after three rings, and he sounded just as distracted as he had the last time she called him. She knew he wasn't there with a woman, so what exactly was he up to?

"Hi, Derek, it's Maddy," she said. "I got your message, and I'm so glad you agree with me. I wanted to crawl out of the community center when I remembered why I had come in the first place. All those people were there to fight homelessness, and I was there hoping to meet men."

"So you didn't even try?" he asked.

"Not at all. But I did sign up to volunteer at a shelter kitchen on Wednesday nights. And who knows, maybe I'll meet someone along the way. But I don't think we should condone this kind of behavior in our columns."

"Neither do I. I wouldn't mind filling up the churches in this city, or getting more people involved, but I want people to act out of the right motives, not turn something good into just another cheap singles bar." The depth of feeling in his voice surprised her. She had never thought of him as the passionate type. It would have been interesting to see how he would have acted at the meeting that night.

"I'm so glad we agree on this. And I could kill Rhona for coming up with this assignment."

He chuckled. "Don't worry, I won't kill you for roping me into this. But you will have to make it up to me somehow."

She sighed. "If you think it's bad now, just wait until our identities are revealed, and everyone in Dallas knows what losers we are."

"I hope that at the same time, someone in the sports world will do something really stupid and crazy so all the radio callers will have something to talk about other than my social life."

She laughed. "I can't wait to see your column on this."

"Yeah, likewise. See you later, Mad Hatter."

*Hers:*

I plead with all readers who have a shred of decency: Don't join a political group or religious organization as a way of meeting people. If these are things that interest you, fine, go ahead and join. Who knows, eventually you may meet someone. But if you do go, check your motives before you walk through the door or you'll feel cheap and degraded.

There's plenty of good to be done by getting involved, and I'm sure that, given time, shared involvement in an organization devoted to helping others would make a wonderful basis for a relationship. In the constraints of this assignment, I don't have time to let something like that develop. I did sign up for some volunteer work, so if something does develop in the next few months, I'll let you know.

But please don't think of this as just another good way to meet people. The people who join these organizations are there because this is something they believe in. They don't have time to waste on people who are there because they can't find meaningful relationships in singles bars.

*His:*

Disclaimer to my mother: I am not telling people not to go to church. I am, however, telling them not to go for the wrong reasons. Like for example, meeting someone of the opposite sex. I'm also not saying church isn't a good place to meet someone and begin a solid relationship. In fact, it's probably the best place to meet someone if you want a deep, committed relationship based on common values.

But if you're only going there to meet people—if the message means nothing to you—you won't have common values. You'll just be an imposter. I'm not saying you'll be struck by lightning if you try this, but I'm pretty sure things won't work out in the end. If the message does mean something to you, you'll immediately feel guilty for having come with the wrong motives.

I'm not going to quit going to church. I'm just not going to go to scope out "church chicks." I may meet a nice girl and develop a relationship, or I may not. But if I do I'll let you know.

# 5

*You go to the mall to buy clothes, gifts and house-
wares. But you might also be able to pick up that
special someone while you're there.*

*But don't go to your usual haunts. Try shopping
in a store aimed at the opposite sex. Go there looking for a gift for your "brother" or "sister." Then,
of course, when you see the right person, he or she
will be just the right size to see if the "gift" will fit
your sibling. Or you could ask for some advice to
help you pick out the perfect gift. That's a surefire
icebreaker because everyone loves to give their
opinions!*

Derek didn't often venture into the mall. He didn't consider shopping a form of recreation. When he needed
something, he went to the store that carried the item, found
the item, bought it and left. It was so much easier to go to
an ordinary store than to fight the crowds at the mall just to
get to one store for one item. But to find women, he'd have
to start at the mall. From the way he heard women talk, he
gathered that the mall was like an amusement park for
women who thought of shopping as fun.

He entered the mall at the entrance near the movie theater—the only entrance he was familiar with. Straight ahead on the main court were several shops that might appeal to women. There was a gourmet shop, but he rejected that one. It wasn't too likely he'd find someone there his own age. A bath and beauty supply store was a possibility, but it would be difficult to ask someone what size might work in there. He decided against the clothing store because he had no idea what was in style right now, and the place looked like it catered to teenagers.

Then he noticed the lingerie store next to the movie theater. He had heard women at work discussing shopping there, and they always got excited when they had packages delivered from their catalog. It was as good a place as any to start, he thought. Judging from the exterior, with ornate windows full of lacy things, he was sure this was a store that catered to the opposite sex. There probably wasn't a socket wrench or screwdriver in the whole place.

Before he got through the door, a rich, floral scent assaulted his nostrils. Yes, this was definitely the right place. It even smelled like a woman. Strains of classical music tinkled in the background, providing the perfect setting for the frilly concoctions that filled the store.

His first instinct was to run away and hope he could go against the grain by finding the perfect woman in the tool department of Sears. Then he noticed the attractive women shopping in the store and changed his mind. He fingered the silky fabric of the nightgown that hung in front of him and worked on a strategy.

This could get tricky. If he asked for help to find a gift, the women were likely to think he was in a relationship intimate enough for him to be buying sexy underwear for a woman. He couldn't imagine buying his sister much of anything in the store. Even though he knew she was an adult, he still pictured her in flannel nightshirts decorated with hearts and teddy bears.

He studied the nightgown he was fingering. The silken fabric flowed over his fingers, and he could imagine how it might drape a woman's body. A vivid image formed in his mind of Maddy, the silk of the nightgown skimming her gentle curves. She wore black all the time, but the pale grayish blue of the nightgown would suit her better, he thought. And the style was definitely her, with its simple, elegant lines. She wasn't the frilly sort. *I wonder what kind of hat she'd wear with this,* he thought, lifting the nightgown on its hanger from the rack.

"Can I help you?" He looked up to see a saleswoman eyeing him, an eyebrow raised in suspicion.

He froze. *Where did that come from?* he wondered. Since when was he thinking of Maddy when he was supposed to be out meeting women? He replaced the nightgown on the rack and hastily dropped his hand to his side. The denim of his jeans seemed uncomfortably rough after the smoothness of the silk.

"I, um, well, I'm looking for a gift for someone," he stammered, feeling his cheeks grow warm. The saleswoman probably thought he was some kind of pervert who was into ladies' underwear, he thought, then decided that he was being a bit paranoid. He was sure men shopped there all the time.

Her eyebrows arched. "Oh? Is it a special occasion? We have some gorgeous teddies on sale."

Derek wasn't sure exactly what a teddy was, but he was pretty sure she had the wrong impression. Not that he blamed her, after the thoughts that had been going through his mind. "It's not that kind of gift," he hastened to explain. "It's my sister's birthday, and she always talks about loving the stuff in this store, so I thought I'd get something here for her.''

"Did you have anything particular in mind?" she asked, with a glance toward the nightgown he had been holding, as if to say that he didn't look like someone shopping for his sister.

He sized up the saleswoman. She was attractive in a tall, lean, blond sort of way, not really his type, but good enough. And she wasn't wearing a wedding or engagement ring. He favored her with his best grin as he struggled to regain some of his composure. "I really have no idea. Maybe you could suggest some things?"

She whirled into action, showing him a selection of nightshirts, bathrobes and nightgowns. He was even more confused than before, and his eyes kept straying to the items of lingerie a man would never buy his sister. He wasn't sure how some of them worked. A few of the contraptions looked like they required engineering degrees in order to just put them on. They certainly didn't look comfortable.

He was dying to ask the saleswoman what they were for, but he'd only just barely rescued himself from looking like a pervert. He wasn't about to risk it again. Besides, he didn't think Maddy would bother with something like that. She was so down-to-earth that he couldn't see her spending extra money on something that was very likely to be taken off quickly, anyway.

There he went, with those thoughts again. He forced himself to return his eyes to the saleswoman.

She was focused on her work and not paying him the least bit of attention as a person, so he could count her out, he decided, even if she didn't think he was some kind of weirdo. He glanced around the store to see if any of the other women there would be good prospects. One of them could turn out to be just his "sister's" size, and he could ask her if he was purchasing the proper fit. But one of the women gushed to her friend about which gown she would wear on her wedding night, and another woman was joined by an impatient-looking man, who gave Derek a funny look for being in the store by himself.

In other words, he'd struck out again. And he had to get out of the store fast, before his runaway imagination took things one step further. He already had Maddy going to bed naked in his mind. If he wasn't careful, soon he'd be in there with her.

He picked out a pink nightshirt trimmed in lace, which he was sure his real sister would love, and bought it, then hurried out of the store as if the gray-blue silk nightgown itself was chasing him. Safely out in the center court, he paused to catch his breath and glance around. It would be just his luck if he ran into one of the Dallas Cowboy football players here. They'd never let him forget it.

He folded the bag over and tucked it under his arm so the logo wouldn't show. He wasn't sure if he was going to kill Maddy for getting him into this, or ask her what some of the things he saw in the store were for. Then again, he'd probably better avoid the topic. He was almost afraid of what his mind would come up with next regarding Maddy and lingerie.

Maddy had never ventured into a sporting goods store in her life. Her idea of exercise was dancing the night away, but this was one place she was sure to find men, and men with good bodies, at that. She was also sure she would have plenty of questions to ask about the merchandise. She could tell a tennis racket from a golf club and a basketball from a football, but that was the extent of her sports knowledge.

A tall, dark and handsome man was perusing the tennis racket display, so she went there first. She picked up a couple of rackets while she thought of a reasonable-sounding question to ask him. Before she could speak, a store employee was at her side. "Is there anything I can help you with? We're having a special on tennis rackets today." He indicated the racket she held. "That's our championship model with the extra-size head and the graphite frame."

She was sure she was supposed to be impressed, so she nodded and said, "Oh? That's wonderful. Too bad I really don't need another racket today. Thank you, anyway, though." She left him there and moved on to the weight benches, where a husky man was checking out the selection.

This time, she didn't have to think of a question. It was on the tip of her tongue when another friendly employee popped out of the woodwork and asked if he could help her. The husky man moved out of range, and she fought to hold back her frustrated sigh. Of all the times she had complained about lackluster service in stores, she had to stumble upon the one place with a friendly, knowledgeable, helpful staff—just when she wanted to rely on other customers for help.

She managed to brush off that employee with only a little effort and moved on to the clothing department. There she was free to look over the selection, but there weren't any men available. They had some interesting spandex leotards on sale, she noticed, and picked one up. It was a startling metallic silver, and it would look great with her black skirt. Something might as well come of this little adventure, she thought as she headed to the register.

She couldn't believe she had failed so miserably in the store. She had been so sure she could find someone like Derek there. After all, he was sort of a jock type.

But did he hang out in sporting goods stores? She closed her eyes and tried to summon up an image of Derek. He wasn't in a sporting goods store, or a hardware store. She strained her imagination, but still couldn't quite place him. Maybe she didn't know him as well as she thought she did.

Why was she thinking about him, anyway? she wondered as she paid for the leotard and left the store. She wasn't trying to find Derek. She knew exactly where he was: in her hair or on her back, just as he had been since she'd known him. So, she didn't need to worry about where she might find him.

On her way out of the mall she spotted a Victoria's Secret store and couldn't resist going in. She always felt feminine in these shops, with their soft scent and elegant music. A pale grayish blue silk gown caught her eye, and she touched it longingly, luxuriating in the feel of the silk against her skin. If only her paycheck allowed her to buy something there, but she had already blown her budget buying the leotard. Someday she was going to buy one of those slinky things, but it would be nicer if she had someone to show it to.

That wouldn't happen unless she got busy, she reminded herself. She wasn't about to meet an unattached man in a Victoria's Secret, unless it happened to be someone else who had read the book. With a sigh, she left the store and strolled through the mall, pausing every so often to window shop. The tobacco shop could be interesting, but then again, you never knew about men who were into that kind of thing.

She passed the toy store reluctantly. She loved going into toy stores, but it was likely that any man in there either had kids or was suffering from a severe Peter Pan complex. She slowed as she passed the record store. A music lover might be fun, but after glancing at the customers, she decided to forego that. She didn't go for high school students, and although she didn't mind earrings and long hair, there was something about a man who had longer hair and wore more jewelry than she did that she found unappealing. Tattoos weren't exactly her cup of tea, either.

The bookstore was a possibility, she thought as she paused in front of the bestsellers display. She wandered aimlessly through the store, finding plenty of books she wanted to read, but no men she wanted to meet—at least none who were alone. When had going to the bookstore become a dating activity?

But the bookstore seemed right, somehow. Like it might be a place she would find what she was looking for. She had learned long ago to trust her intuition, so she waited a while longer, pausing in her favorite sections, but no one interesting showed up.

She had already exceeded her budget and her feet hurt, so she reluctantly decided to call it quits. Hanging out in the mall had been great when she was in high school, but somehow it didn't seem the thing to do now that she was an adult. If she didn't have any luck later, she could always check out that huge hardware store near downtown, she thought. The place was bound to be crawling with men. She wondered where Derek had gone shopping, and if he had done better than she had.

*Hers:*

Shopping for a man at the mall is a lot like shopping for anything else at the mall. You have to have a good idea of what you want to find, you have to know what suits you, you have to know where to find it, and you have to be able to compare so you'll know you got the best of all possible selections. Frankly, I'd rather apply these skills to finding a great pair of shoes.

For one thing, men move around too much. You

can't spot a great man in a store one week, then look around a bit and later go back and get the first one you saw when you decide he's the best one, after all. Men also don't advertise when they're going to be there.

I made the mistake of going to a store with friendly, well-trained, helpful employees. If I ever really need sporting goods, I'll go back there, but they made it impossible for me to approach any of the customers for advice. A quick sweep through the mall didn't turn up any other prospects. Maybe I just picked a bad day. There must have been a basketball game on TV.

Like most of the advice in this book, this method relies far too much on serendipity, and who needs advice on how to be lucky?


*His:*

It's obvious that a woman wrote this book. Describing hunting for a mate as shopping is a good clue. Most men don't look at shopping as a form of recreation. It's a bothersome chore, usually put off until the last possible minute. Then we don't have time to "shop." We just go where we know we'll find what we need, get it and get out.

This shopping technique might work if we knew we could find the perfect woman in a certain place at a certain time, but most of us don't have the patience to wander around a shopping mall, hoping to run into a woman we find attractive.

I wouldn't suggest a lingerie shop as a starting point for men who want to try this. The only men I saw in the store were with women, and they weren't too happy about being there. They looked at me rather suspiciously. I used the excuse of looking for something for my sister, but that limited my selections to chaste nightgowns, which don't leave much room for asking advice from anyone.

If you really do have a sister, get her advice before you hit the mall. She can tell you the best places to shop if you want to meet women. Better yet, take her shopping. Then you can smile indulgently, as you have the perfect excuse for being in the women's department. My own sister was horrified that I went to Victoria's Secret alone. She was the one who suggested I take her shopping. Even if she did have an ulterior motive, I think it sounds like a good idea.

# 6

"Go-o-d Mo-o-orning, Da-a-a-allas," boomed the voice on the radio. "Have you seen the *Journal* this morning? It seems our intrepid newspaper pair have yet another adventure to report. I just wonder when they're going to give us something really juicy."

Maddy quit brushing her teeth long enough to change the radio dial. It was bad enough to have to put herself through the humiliation of this assignment. She didn't want to have to listen to other people discussing her.

"Say, how about those losers at the *Journal?*" the new station's disk jockey said. "It kind of makes you wonder if those two could get a date if you threw them into a throng of desperate singles. I can't wait to read about their next adventure."

Maddy changed the dial again. The classical station should be safe, she thought. The symphony, or whatever it was they were playing, crashed to a big finish. There was a long pause, then the well-modulated voice of the announcer gave the name of the piece, the composer and the orchestra. After another long pause, the announcer said, "And have you been reading the life-style section of the *Journal* lately? I wonder if those two have thought of joining the symphony's singles organization. They might have some luck there."

With a deep groan, Maddy switched off the radio. She couldn't escape from it. She dreaded the time when their identities were revealed. So far, it was still a secret at the paper, but the staff were trying to guess. With such a small staff, it was only a matter of time before they figured it out. Then Maddy knew she was in for some serious ribbing. She wondered if the federal witness-protection program might have provisions for people like her.

But Rhona had been right. People were interested, and the columns were selling papers. All over the city, people were talking about the book and the newspaper columns. The book was selling better than ever, despite the reporters' lack of success at following its advice, and the author had challenged the reporters to a debate on a local television talk show. Rhona was beside herself with joy.

Despite the success, though, Maddy was feeling down. Her lack of success in the dating scene had never bothered her before. She just assumed that at the right time, the right person would come along. She felt that somehow she was testing fate by looking for "Mr. Right," and she was being punished with failure. Even the things she normally enjoyed doing became joyless when she had to keep her agenda constantly in mind. Her volunteer work at the soup kitchen was the only good thing to come out of the assignment so far.

As she headed to work, Maddy wondered how Derek was feeling. He was even more reserved than she was, and he hadn't had any success at all, so far. Not that it would do any good even if both of them complained of severe depression brought on by the assignment. Management was fully behind the whole project, now that it was selling papers and making money.

As soon as she arrived at work Rhona met her at the door to the newsroom with a rib-crushing hug. "You're wonderful!'' she exclaimed. ''Did you hear the radio this morning?''

Maddy grimaced and glanced around the newsroom to see if anyone else had noticed. Rhona was going to blow her cover if she didn't calm down. ''Unfortunately—'' Maddy sighed ''—they're calling me a loser.''

Rhona dismissed her concerns with a wave of her hand. ''They don't really mean that. They're just being funny.''

''But they're saying it on the radio. Thousands of people are hearing it. Then when they find out who I am, all those people will think I'm a loser. And Derek, too.''

''No, they won't,'' Rhona assured her as she tucked a strand of her hair—it was red today—behind her ear. ''By then you'll have reported that you've found someone wonderful. They won't remember the bad times at the beginning.''

Maddy trudged to her desk, leaving Rhona to follow behind her. ''It's not the beginning anymore, Rhona,'' she told her editor. ''We're more than halfway through the book.''

''But you only need one suggestion to work. That could be the next one.''

''We'll see,'' Maddy sighed as she sat at her desk and pulled the book out of her knapsack.

Rhona patted her on the shoulder. ''Everything will be okay, you'll see. Management may even have something special for you when this is done, it's been so successful.''

''Can they send me to Eastern Europe?'' Maddy muttered under her breath as the editor whisked back to her office. She returned her attention to the book.

*To have a good life relationship, or even a good dating relationship, you need to have something in common with each other. Mutual interests automatically give you a topic for conversation and something to do to-*

*gether.*

*One way to find someone who shares your interests is to join a hobby club, for example, a "Star Trek" fan club or a stamp collecting club. Or you could find a community education class in a subject that interests you. If you're lucky, you may find someone with whom you can practice what you've learned!*

Maddy dropped the book on her desk with a sigh. Actually, this advice shouldn't be too difficult to act on, and it could even be fun. At any rate, it shouldn't make her feel guilty. She pulled open a file drawer and began digging. A few weeks ago she had received a catalog for an adult-education program. She had filed it away, with the intention of doing a story about it. The program was supposed to be a hot spot for singles.

She finally found it, filed, oddly enough, under *S* for *Singles*. The course selection included everything from arts to new age spiritualism to careers. She flipped through the catalog, looking for something that sparked her interest, and which might also attract some men. Most of the cooking classes were probably not a good idea, and neither were the crafts classes.

Then she saw a listing that looked like fun, and which would allow her to make some use of the expensive graduation present her grandparents had given her when she finished college. She picked up the phone and called in her registration.

Derek slouched into his seat in the café, trying to be inconspicuous. Even though he knew his identity as the "his" part of the romance columns was still secret, he felt self-conscious because everywhere he went, people were talking about him. Worst of all, he hadn't written much of anything worthwhile in his novel in the four weeks since the assignment began.

"Oh, hi!" Maddy's voice jolted him out of his pity party. "We need to talk."

"Yeah, we do," he said, sitting up a little straighter. "Have a seat."

She put her tray on the table and took a seat. "Is this thing driving you crazy, too?" she asked.

"Good, I'm not the only one," he said with a relieved smile. "I thought I was just feeling sorry for myself."

"You're just upset because you're behind," she said with a smug grin as she popped a forkful of salad into her mouth.

He shook his head. "Uh-uh. We're still even. Remember, it's three dates with the same person, not three dates total. Now, if you want to find the accountant guy for another date..." He let the insinuation hang as his voice trailed off.

She shuddered. "No, thanks. I don't have his number, and he doesn't have mine, even if I wanted to find him again."

"That bad, huh?"

"Worse. I toned it down in the column in case he recognized the situation. I didn't want him suing me for libel."

"Truth is a good defense for libel, you know."

She smiled. "Then I'd be off the hook as soon as the jury was around him longer than ten minutes."

They both laughed, and Derek's melancholy eased in the presence of her good humor. He had always felt comfortable around Maddy, when he wasn't thinking about lingerie. He forced that thought out of his head and asked, "So, what form of torture do we have to put ourselves through this time?"

"This one should be fun. We get to take a class in something that interests us."

He groaned. "Maddy, I don't have time for that kind of thing. I'm already working two jobs."

"You don't have to go to graduate school. You can take an adult-education class for fun. Most of the classes just meet a couple of times. Some only meet once. Surely you'll find something you like." She bent and fished around in her knapsack, then came up with a catalog and handed it to him. "Here, take a look through this and pick something. You can keep it. I've already registered for my class."

He looked at the catalog warily. The cover promised courses that would help him get his life together, get a better job, be more interesting and have better relationships. It sounded too good to be true. He flipped through the booklet, then put it aside to peruse later. Bracing his elbows on the table, he leaned forward and studied Maddy.

He wondered how she really felt about what they were doing. His mental image of her had always been of a party girl with a lot of friends who never spent a Saturday night at home. This assignment wouldn't be much of a change of pace for her, then. He wondered if he'd formed a stereotype without really knowing her.

"What do you think about this assignment?" he asked.

"I kind of think it's degrading. And I hate having my social life be the topic of discussion all over town."

"But what about the things we're doing? Would you enjoy them if we didn't have to write about them?"

She tossed lettuce around her salad bowl with her fork as she frowned in thought. Finally she said, "It's not the things we're doing that I mind so much as the agenda we have to keep in mind while we're doing them. Not that I would normally be doing all these things, but having to try them has been good for me. That is, except for the grocery store and the sporting goods store. I could have done without those. What about you?"

This time it was his turn to think. "I didn't really like the nightclubs—either of them. That's just not me. And neither was Victoria's Secret."

Maddy giggled. "I've been trying to picture you in there. That must have been funny."

He could feel his face growing warm. "Yeah, I guess it was. Someday you'll have to explain some of those things in that store to me. I'm curious." He left out any reference to how she and silk nightgowns were now forever linked in his brain. She might take that the wrong way.

"The next catalog I get, I'll talk you through it in private," she promised. "I won't make you go back to the store."

"When I got home, I even took a shower because I smelled all perfumey."

She laughed again, and her grey-green eyes sparkled with mirth. "You're really not enjoying this, are you. Have you ever thought that it might be good for you to get out of your comfort zone?"

"It wouldn't be so bad if I felt I was accomplishing anything. Mostly I just feel like I'm wasting my time. You should have picked someone else for this."

She reached across the table and laid her hand on his. "I think you were the perfect person to pick. We're both difficult cases. If this were easy for us, we wouldn't need the book. We'd have found someone on our own."

He looked down to see her hand resting on his, then looked up at her. She looked back at him, square in the eye, and gave him a little smile. The table between them seemed to have shrunk, drawing them closer together. He was acutely conscious of the feel of her cool, smooth hand on his. Seemingly oblivious to the sensations that were churning through him, she smiled again, gave his hand a squeeze and went back to eating her lunch.

"Anyway," she said, "we're almost through with the book. Then we can put all this behind us and go back to our normal lives. I can go out just to dance and won't have to try a new social event every week, and you can go back to doing whatever it is you like to do." She cocked her head at him. "What do you do when you're all by yourself all weekend?"

"Half the year, I'm not home by myself all weekend. The Cowboys play football on Sundays, and I'm at all the games. The rest of the year, I'm catching up on the things I didn't do during football season." He hoped that satisfied her. He liked Maddy, and in the past few weeks they had become closer friends, but he still wasn't ready to tell her everything about himself. The last thing she needed was something else to tease him about.

She already had plenty of material. With a wicked grin, she leaned across the table. "So, you sports guys actually have to do some real work from time to time. Imagine, having to give up your weekends to fly on chartered jets, stay in nice hotels and go to football games. Must be rough."

"For our next project," he retorted, "we can switch jobs. I'll go to all the concerts for free, and you can spend every other weekend alone in a strange city."

"Ooh, sounds like fun." She glanced at her watch, then gasped. "Speaking of which, I've got to get back to the newsroom. I wouldn't want to miss a minute of writing those exciting personality profiles, would I?" She picked up her knapsack and dashed out the door.

Derek watched her go, suddenly aware that he had relaxed as soon as she left the room. He wondered for a moment about what that meant, then shrugged and picked up the catalog Maddy had left. He thumbed through it, looking for something that interested him, preferably a class with only one or two meetings. The music section had a number of one-day seminars, but he didn't care to spend a Sunday afternoon listening to opera or organ music from the Baroque period. The pop psychology courses would probably be full of people looking for healthy relationships, but they would probably all be trying to get over something.

He was interested in the class on selling a novel, but he'd worry about that one when he finished his book. He flipped past the rest of the arts classes, then turned back when an illustration caught his eye. It was a photo of a bird in flight, silhouetted against the sky. The photo illustrated the description of a class on nature photography. It only met twice, on Friday evenings two weeks apart. The first meeting was to discuss techniques, then participants were to try what they learned, and the second meeting was to critique photographs.

That didn't seem like too much of a time commitment, and Derek had learned photography when working for his high school newspaper and yearbook. He had become quite good at capturing athletes in motion. It might be interesting to try capturing wildlife in motion. The class began the coming Friday night, so he still had time to register. He folded down a corner of the catalog's page to mark the place. He had a good feeling about this tactic. His luck was bound to change this time.

# 7

Maddy had almost forgotten what the first day of school felt like, but this experience was giving her a good reminder. She hurried down the hall of the community center, scanning the room numbers on the doors for the right room. She was running late, and her hands were sweaty as she clutched her new spiral notebook. Just like when she had been in grade school, she hoped her new teacher was nice and that she'd find a friend in the class.

The teacher was still distributing handouts when Maddy found the classroom. There were about fifteen people in the room, most of them young, professional-looking people in their twenties or thirties, with one older couple. It looked as though several of the others in the class were part of couples, which immediately reduced her odds. But her hopes rose when she noticed the tall blonde with broad shoulders who sat in the front row. Braving stares from the teacher and the other students, she overcame her instinct to slip into the back row and instead marched to the front of the room and took a seat next to the blonde.

Then she turned around and wished she could crawl back out of the room. "Derek Newman, what the hell are you doing here?" she hissed.

He looked equally stunned to see her. "I'm taking this class," he whispered back.

She shook her head. "You're spying on me, aren't you. You're following me."

"I was here first," he pointed out. "You came in after me."

"But I registered first."

"Did it ever occur to you that we might accidentally have something in common and just happened to choose the same class?" he asked, but she couldn't reply because the instructor stopped by her desk to give her a handout.

She flipped through the photocopied sheets, all the while studying Derek out of the corner of her eye. It really never had occurred to her that they might have anything in common. She had always considered him her direct opposite—athletic, traditional and reserved.

Not that both of them taking a nature photography class automatically meant they had much of anything in common. She wasn't that interested in nature photography. She just happened to have a very nice camera her grandparents had given her, and she wanted to learn something beyond the basics so she could take real pictures with some creativity. For all she knew, he was an avid nature photographer whose home was filled with pictures of deer and birds. She wouldn't be surprised.

Now that she knew the gorgeous blonde was just Derek, she wished she had chosen a different seat. Sitting in the front row made it difficult to check out the other class participants while the instructor was talking. When the instructor finished going over the handout and dimmed the lights to show slides, she managed to glance around the room.

Even with the lights down, the prospects weren't exciting. As she had suspected, most of the men in the room were there as parts of couples. The unattached men, other than Derek, looked like they actually thought it would be fun to get up before dawn to huddle in damp bushes and wait for a yellow-bellied sapsucker to fly by. That was not *her* idea of a good time.

While she was at it, she also checked to see what kind of women were there so she could guess at which one Derek might go for. There was one attractive blonde. She looked like the cheerleader type, the kind who might attract a former star athlete. Together, she and Derek would look like Ken and Barbie. It was enough to make Maddy gag.

Unable to bear the thought, she returned her attention to the slides. After a few minutes, she was even able to join the discussion as the class participants and the instructor analyzed each photograph. By the end of the class, she was eager to try her hand at taking photographs.

The instructor gave them the assignment of shooting a roll of film, having it developed and bringing their best photos to the next meeting. He encouraged them to form teams within the class. Maddy waited for Derek to approach the blonde, but instead he walked out of the classroom with Maddy. "What do you say we form a team?" he asked.

"You and me? Are you forgetting why we're here?"

He shook his head and grimaced. "I'm not all that interested in anyone here. I figure I'll just cut my losses and work with someone I know I can have fun with."

Maddy felt her cheeks grow pink. She wasn't used to him complimenting her like this. She didn't even know that he thought favorably of her. Normally he was finding new ways to tease her. "Okay," she said. "You're right about the lack of prospects. Maybe we just chose the wrong class."

"Better the wrong class that we enjoy, anyway, than the wrong class that's a bore."

"And you were the one who first accused me of not really wanting to try on this assignment."

"Are you doing anything tomorrow afternoon?" he asked. "We could go out to White Rock Lake and take some pictures."

She paused and considered. This sounded suspiciously like she was being asked out on a date. She wondered if it counted if they went out with each other. Then she had to bite her lip to keep from laughing. This was Derek, whom she'd known for years. It wasn't a date, it was just making the best of a bad situation. "That sounds great," she said.

"Good. I'll pick you up around noon. We can get a take-out lunch and spend the afternoon working."

"Okay," she said. They had reached her car, and she leaned against the door. "I need to get some film, though. I'll probably need a few rolls just to get the hang of things. I haven't used my camera much. It may take me a while to remember what an f-stop is."

"Don't worry, I can help you with that."

"So you really do know about photography?"

"I've done some, just not artistic photography. I can shoot a basketball game pretty well, though."

She nodded. "Oh, I never knew that about you." An awkward silence followed her remark. There was a lot about him she didn't know, and she realized that she wouldn't mind learning more. She looked at him for a moment, then turned and unlocked her door when he didn't say anything in response. "Well, I guess I'd better be going. I'll see you tomorrow."

He took a step toward her, paused, then backed away. "Yeah, see you tomorrow at noon." He had turned and walked to his truck before she got her engine started.

It might not be a real date, she thought as she drove home, but she felt more jittery about this outing than she had about her high school senior prom. This assignment was making her crazy.

* * *

Maddy still had butterflies in her stomach as she got dressed the next morning. Reminding herself that it wasn't a date, she started with faded jeans, a T-shirt with a denim shirt worn over it and old tennis shoes. Then she worried that might not be right and changed into a newer pair of jeans and a nicer shirt. She looked nicer, but that outfit would be silly for trekking through underbrush. She had just changed back into the original outfit and topped it off with a baseball cap when there was a knock at her door.

Derek stood there, wearing equally scruffy jeans and an old polo shirt—and looking better than she had ever seen him, for some odd reason. "Ready?" he asked.

"Just a second." She grabbed her camera bag and latched her fanny pack around her waist. After locking the door behind herself, she tucked her key into the pack.

They took Derek's truck, and he navigated across town to the lake, stopping at a deli along the way to pick up sandwiches. The lake was an incongruous urban oasis in the middle of Dallas. Derek parked near a picnic area, where they ate lunch with a minimum of conversation as children ran past. Frisbees whipped overhead and a nearby boom box blasted Rap music at a volume that made the picnic table vibrate. Maddy didn't know what to say to him, and she enjoyed the quick camaraderie between them more than she felt the need to make conversation. Derek seemed lost in his own world, his mind apparently focused on a faraway problem.

He looked so pensive Maddy had to ask, "What is it, Derek?"

He jumped, then smiled sheepishly and said, "Sorry, I just started thinking."

"About what?"

He shrugged, not meeting her eye. "Nothing much. I was just trying to remember where we might find some good places to get some pictures. A springtime Saturday probably isn't the best time for us to come here to escape civilization."

"There are different kinds of wildlife, you know."

He smiled, and the tension left his face. "But most of them don't photograph too well. Imagine showing off a picture of fraternity boys at the next class and trying to convince the instructor they're another form of wildlife."

"Do you have any other ideas, then?"

He studied her for a moment, then said, "How adventurous are you feeling?"

"You know me. I'm always ready for adventure."

"I know this place out in Irving, near the Trinity River. It's civilized enough to have a walking trail, but it's almost deserted."

If this had been any other man she had met through a class, she would have immediately become suspicious when he suggested going to an almost-deserted place in the river valley, but this was Derek. She knew she could trust him with her life, if necessary. "Okay. You're driving," she said.

He got up from the table and gathered their trash from lunch. "Then, let's go." He dropped the trash in a garbage can on the edge of the picnic grounds, then led the way back to his truck.

To get to Derek's wilderness, they had to drive all the way across Dallas and into the suburb of Irving. About halfway to their destination, Maddy reached her tolerance limit for country music and changed the radio station dial to her favorite station, which played alternative music.

"Hey!" Derek protested.

"I'm sorry, but I can't take much more crying in the beer because my dog got run over by a pickup truck."

"I don't know that this monotone, socially conscious whining is any better."

"Okay, then. Let's see if we can find something we can agree on." She found an oldies rock and roll station, and they both agreed they could tolerate that for a while. Derek rolled down the truck's windows, and Maddy let the wind whip her hair around her face. It didn't get much better than this, cruising down the road on a warm spring afternoon, with Buddy Holly on the radio and the wind in her hair.

"What are you smiling about?" Derek's voice didn't break the spell of contentment that surrounded her. Rather, it only added to the effect. He had been perceptive enough to notice her pleasure, and that earned him high marks in her book.

"This is nice" was all she said.

He nodded. "Yeah, it is. It makes me realize I work too hard."

She leaned her head back against the seat and smiled dreamily. "Remember when you were a teenager, and doing something like this would be the ultimate? Imagine, being able to go where you want to when you want to, and not have to be home at any particular time. We could stay out all night if we wanted to. Now we don't even think about it anymore, we take our freedom for granted."

"I'll admit, that was the hardest thing for me to get used to as an adult, not having to account to anyone for my time or money. Sometimes I still think I try to justify everything I do, and I don't know who I'm trying to please."

"And do you ever come up with reasons or excuses for staying up too late at night?"

He laughed. "So I'm not the only one!"

"You need to loosen up more, Newman." She opened her eyes to watch him as he drove. He studied the road with intense concentration, both hands gripping the steering wheel.

She wondered if he ever really relaxed, and what he would be like if he did. The more she was around him, the more she knew about him, and the more she wanted to know. There were so many layers to peel through before she could find the real Derek. Back in college, she never would have guessed that the handsome jock could be so complex.

They left the city behind and entered a no-man's land between cities. The towers of the Las Colinas development beckoned ahead of them, but Derek turned to go in the opposite direction and pulled into a small patch of gravel that served as a parking lot. A wooden sign there informed them that this was a greenbelt recreational area. All Maddy could see was a dirt path, some tall grass, a small lake and some trees—not exactly her idea of recreation. She kind of liked the comforting feel of pavement under her feet.

Derek picked up his camera bag and slung it over his shoulder, and Maddy did the same. He stepped easily over the chain that separated the parking area from the park, then extended a hand to help her across. When she was safely on the other side, he retained his hold on her hand. Her hand felt small and fragile in the firm grasp of his larger hand. She let him lead the way as, hand in hand, they crossed the mowed, parklike grass to the dirt hiking path.

The farther they went down the path, the more remote and wild the area seemed. When they went below the hill, Maddy could no longer see the road. The going got harder as they trudged through tall grass and weeds to the lake's shore. Maddy was grateful that Derek was leading the way to navigate them through the foliage. Eventually, they reached an outcropping of rocks on the shore.

"Here we are," Derek said with a deep, contented sigh and a squeeze of Maddy's hand. She had to admit it was rather nice. The lake was small enough that the two of them could probably walk its perimeter in just a few hours. It seemed to have been formed when the not-too-distant river had once overflowed its banks, then receded. Marshy grasses rimmed the lake and filled the shallows. Across the lake, on the opposite shore, trees clustered, some bending to dip their branches in the still water.

As she gazed at the sunlight-dappled water, Maddy hoped she could capture a fraction of the image on film. "This is nice," she breathed, giving Derek's hand an answering squeeze and wishing she could come up with something to say that better described her feelings. She couldn't just keep repeating "This is nice" all day.

But Derek didn't seem to notice that she was repeating herself. The two of them stood silently for a few more moments. Maddy felt a bond between them she had never noticed before. Had it always been there and she just hadn't noticed, or had it formed recently?

Before she could determine the answer, Derek released her hand and bent to place his camera bag on one of the rocks. He took his camera out of the bag and slung its strap around his neck. She followed his lead, then attempted to photograph the scene before her before the moment was lost. Something told her she might want to remember this later.

She tried all the techniques she could remember from the class, using the light to create effects and framing the shot to give a sense of proportion and balance. Still, she preferred to capture it with her eyes. Then she would be sure of a truer image of what this meant to her.

Derek was snapping away, making gradual adjustments to the camera as he went along. Somewhat intimidated in the presence of such expertise, she returned to framing her shot, focusing and shooting one picture at a time. She had just begun falling into a sort of rhythm when Derek interrupted her with a gentle touch on her arm.

"Don't make a sudden move, but turn around very slowly and quietly," he whispered under his breath.

She did as he said, then had to bite her tongue to keep from crying out in pleasure. A beautiful white bird had perched on a rock in the lake, no more than ten feet from where they stood. Slowly and carefully, she moved her camera back to her eye and squeezed off a couple of quick shots in case the bird flew away, then she tried changing the focus for a tighter shot. She was only just getting started when the bird flew away. Derek followed its flight with his camera, shooting quickly, but she wasn't ambitious enough to try to capture motion.

"What was that?" she asked when the bird was out of sight.

"An egret," he said. "We had them often enough around my parents' farm, but I think this might have been a slightly different kind. I'm no expert on birds."

"You're better than I am. I do well to identify Tweety Bird." She glanced around the lake, then asked, "Do you think we'll see any more wildlife?"

"I have no idea. It just depends on what shows up. I'm not too familiar with this place. I just drive by here every so often and I was curious about exploring."

His eyes narrowed in concentration as he studied the setting. Then he pointed toward the lake. "See that?" he said.

She looked, and noticed a squiggle disturbing the lake's still waters. "You mean that squiggly thing? What is it?"

"A water snake of some sort. Maybe a cottonmouth."

"A snake!" She fought back a shudder and involuntarily clutched his arm. "It won't come here, will it?"

"I doubt it," he said, not saying anything about her cowardice. For that she was grateful, if a little surprised. Usually, he would take every opportunity to tease her.

"I don't think I'll take a picture of it," she said. "I don't like looking at snakes."

"I don't blame you."

"You don't?" she looked at him, shocked that he had missed such an obvious opening for a witty remark.

"I wouldn't classify cottonmouth snakes as among the creatures I'd like to have hanging on my wall." He bent to pick up his camera bag and took her hand again. "Come on, let's see what else we can find."

She picked up her own bag and followed him around the perimeter of the lake. At first, he was always the one to notice the little details worth photographing, but as they went along, she learned to find them herself. She spotted a squirrel scurrying up a tree, a songbird perched on a slim branch, and in her biggest triumph, she was able to photograph a jackrabbit that had paused for a second.

"I hope that one comes out okay," she said, rising from her knees as the jackrabbit bounded off across the valley. Derek was still shooting it as it ran. She watched him, a smile playing about her lips, then said, "Don't you take pictures of anything sitting still?"

To answer her question, he turned around and took a quick picture of her. "Satisfied?" he asked with a wicked grin. She smiled in return. This was the Derek she knew. "Believe it or not," he added, "I'm better at taking pictures of things as they move than I am at still photography. I think it comes from the fact that I learned photography when I was shooting high school sports. I'm terrible at portraits."

"Well, if the sportswriting thing doesn't work out for you, I bet you could get a job at a portrait studio taking pictures of two-year-olds who can't sit still."

He laughed. "I never thought of it that way. I wonder if that would classify as wildlife. But until then, let's make the most of this light. It gets more interesting as the sun starts going down.''

She shielded her eyes and looked in the general direction of the sun. ''It's not nearly sunset,'' she said.

''But it's past noon, and that means the sun is on its way down. See how the shadows are lengthening? That's when you can get some interesting pictures.''

''Okay, whatever you say, but I'm not staying out here past dark. I want to be able to see where I'm stepping, in case we run into our friend from the lake.''

As if by unspoken agreement, he took her hand again and led her back toward the lake. She noticed that the shadows were lengthening, and she began to see just what the instructor had meant about framing a picture when she saw the interesting angles made between a tree and its shadow. ''Wait up a second, Derek,'' she said, letting go of his hand. ''I want to get this shot.'' She focused carefully, adjusting the aperture for the reduced light, and took a few shots. She was pretty sure it would make a good picture. When she was done, she automatically took his hand again. It was strange just how natural it felt.

He cleared the way for her through the tall grass and underbrush back to the edge of the lake. There, Maddy let out a cry of delight when she saw a mother duck and her baby ducklings parading across the lake's surface. Both Maddy and Derek brought up their cameras to capture the scene. Maddy was surprised to notice the silly grin on Derek's face as he continued to take pictures of the duck family. He was a softy inside that strong, athletic exterior.

''This is really great, Derek,'' she said when he had finished shooting pictures. ''How did you find this place?''

''I drive by it all the time. I live just north of here, and the radio station's down in Las Colinas. I just never had a reason to stop and explore.''

"Well, this was perfect. I think we got just what we needed."

"Do you think you have enough?"

"I shot three rolls of film. We're only supposed to bring a few pictures to class."

"Okay, so I guess we can head back to the truck now."

She hesitated. She didn't need to take any more pictures, and she was out of film, but she didn't want to go home yet. She was enjoying this too much.

Derek solved her dilemma for her. "Or do you want to go get some dinner?"

"Sorry, but I don't have any money with me." And very little in her checking account, to be perfectly honest.

"That's okay. It's my treat."

She couldn't resist a little teasing. "Do you mean this is some kind of date?"

He gave her a wry smile. "If that's what you want to call it, maybe it is. We can at least write about it that way. We don't have to say who we met in the class, or that we went to the same class, but maybe we can get rid of some of the 'loser' stigma."

"Okay then, it's a date. But where can we go dressed like this?" Both of them wore old clothes, and they both looked like they had spent the afternoon slogging through mud and tall grass.

"I know a Mexican place in the boonies with outdoor tables. We might even be overdressed for that."

"Whatever you say. You're the one who's paying." She took his hand again and let him lead her back to the truck.

The radio was still set on the oldies station, so the Beach Boys serenaded them when the truck started. Derek rolled down the windows and drove even farther away from the city. Maddy sang along softly with the radio, letting the wind carry her words away. She couldn't remember the last time she felt this happy, and she wondered if it had anything to do with the man sitting next to her.

# 8

If he had planned for this day to turn out to be a "date," Derek would have chosen another activity that would have required a different wardrobe so they could have gone to a different restaurant. He tried to be a true gentleman on a first date, taking a woman to a nice place suitable for quiet conversation. Rico's Rancho Loco wasn't quite what he would have had in mind.

But this hadn't been planned. That morning when he left home, he had just planned on spending the afternoon taking pictures with Maddy. He wasn't sure when the mood between them had shifted to create such a feeling of intimacy. But he was reluctant to let it go—leading him to suggest dinner, just so they could stay together a little while longer.

As he pulled his truck into the open expanse of dirt that served as the restaurant's parking lot, he was glad he had known Maddy too long to be able to impress her with something as superficial as a choice of restaurants. Rico's Rancho Loco made quite an impression—he just wasn't sure it was one he would want associated with him as a memory of a first evening together.

The restaurant itself was a metal shack that gave the appearance of leaning over to one side. It was draped with strands of Christmas lights, the kind with the big painted bulbs that were visible from the road even when they weren't lit. The strands of lights were strung from the building to poles in front, creating a canopy of light over the restaurant's outdoor patio. Although it was early in the evening, a raucous crowd already filled the patio.

"It may not look like much, but it has passed the health department's inspections, and they make the best enchiladas you'll ever have," Derek assured Maddy as he tried to see the restaurant through her eyes. It was okay for him, but he worried that she might not approve.

He appeared to have underestimated her, though. Her eyes shone with delight and a huge grin lit up her face. "Now, this is what I call atmosphere!" she said. "I'll have to write up a review for the paper."

"I wish you wouldn't. I like it just as it is, where you can only find it if you know about it. Don't let it become popular. They have enough business, anyway."

That proved to be true, for they got the last table left on the patio. Maddy flicked a few crumbs off the dented aluminum table top as she sat down, but her smile hadn't faded. Her shoulders moved in time with the vibrant Mexican polkas playing over the speaker system.

"How did you find this place?" she asked. "I thought you were sort of a homebody."

"The football players eat here all the time, and they dragged me out once."

She glanced around the crowd on the patio and asked, "Like those guys?" as she indicated a table off to the side.

Derek turned to see several members of the Dallas Cowboys gathered around the table, then he waved in response to the shouts of, "Hey, Derek, my man!" that came from the other table.

# SILHOUETTE®

# AN IMPORTANT MESSAGE FROM THE EDITORS OF SILHOUETTE®

Dear Reader,

Because you've chosen to read one of our fine romance novels, we'd like to say "thank you"! And, as a **special** way to thank you, we've selected <u>four more</u> of the <u>books</u> you love so well, **and** a Cuddly Teddy Bear to send you absolutely *FREE!*

Please enjoy them with our compliments...

*[signature]*

Senior Editor,
Silhouette Yours Truly

P.S. And because we value our customers, we've attached something extra inside ...

EDITOR'S
FREE
GIFT
SEAL
THANK YOU

PEEL OFF SEAL AND
PLACE INSIDE

# HOW TO VALIDATE
## YOUR
# EDITOR'S FREE GIFT
# "THANK YOU"

**1.** Peel off gift seal from front cover. Place it in space provided at right. This automatically entitles you to receive four free books and a Cuddly Teddy Bear.

**2.** Send back this card and you'll get brand-new Silhouette Yours Truly™ novels. These books have a cover price of $3.50 each, but they are yours to keep absolutely free.

**3.** There's no catch. You're under no obligation to buy anything. We charge nothing — ZERO — for your first shipment. And you don't have to make any minimum number of purchases — not even one!

**4.** The fact is thousands of readers enjoy receiving books by mail from the Silhouette Reader Service™ months before they're available in stores. They like the convenience of home delivery and they love our discount prices!

**5.** We hope that after receiving your free books you'll want to remain a subscriber. But the choice is yours — to continue or cancel, anytime at all! So why not take us up on our invitation, with no risk of any kind. You'll be glad you did!

**6.** Don't forget to detach your FREE BOOKMARK. And remember...just for validating your Editor's Free Gift Offer, we'll send you FIVE MORE gifts, *ABSOLUTELY FREE!*

© 1991 HARLEQUIN ENTERPRISES LTD.

"Yeah, like those guys," he said, feeling his cheeks grow warm. "You realize now I'll be grilled about you the next time I'm in the locker room."

She propped her elbows on the table and rested her chin in her cupped hands. "And what are you going to tell them?" she asked, with a mischievous glint in her gray-green eyes.

Derek considered her question. His experience with women had shown that to be a question that could get him into big trouble if he answered wrong. The problem was, he wasn't sure of the answer. He had considered her a friend ever since they worked on the school newspaper together in college. Lately, their friendship had deepened. Now he was growing more aware of her as a woman he found intriguing and attractive.

The waitress rescued him from having to form an immediate answer by arriving with water and a basket of tortilla chips with hot sauce, handing them menus and taking their drink orders. They both ordered frozen margaritas, then Maddy apparently forgot her question as she turned her attention to the laminated menu she held. She blindly reached for a chip and dipped it in the sauce, then said, "You said the enchiladas were good."

"The best," he assured her.

She nodded, crunching on the chip. She immediately started coughing and reached for her glass of water. "Oh, my!" she said, wiping away the tears streaming down her face. "If the food's anything like the salsa, this should be good."

"I'm sorry, I should have warned you about the sauce. It's a bit on the spicy side."

"A bit? This stuff should have a warning label." She took another sip of water, then dipped another chip into the sauce. "I guess I'm just a glutton for punishment." This time, her reaction wasn't as severe, only requiring one gulp of water.

The waitress arrived with their drinks and took their orders. They both ordered enchilada dinners. When the waitress left, Maddy stirred her drink, took a sip, then said, "You never did answer my question."

*Uh-oh,* he thought. She wasn't going to let it rest, and he was no closer to an answer. He tried to play innocent. "Which question?"

"Don't try to weasel out of this one, Newman. You know which question. What are you going to say about me to your locker room buddies?"

"What do you want me to say about you?"

She tossed her head back and laughed, then said, "You're wimping out on me. Come on, tell me."

"Well, let's see. I knew you in college when you were a snooty, know-it-all journalism major with high aspirations. I work with you. We're taking a class together and were working on our homework when we decided to get dinner. We aren't sleeping together, and if they're interested, you're not taken so I could set something up."

She threw a tortilla chip at him. "That's it?"

"Hey, I gave you the opportunity to tell me what you wanted me to say, so don't complain." He wondered if he should have added that he found her very attractive and hoped she didn't meet anyone else through the course of this project. No, probably not, he decided. He wasn't prepared for the response if she didn't agree.

The waitress brought their food with a warning that the plates were hot. Maddy scooped up a steaming bite of enchilada and blew on it. Her eyes were focused behind Derek, toward the table full of football players. He assumed she was trying to decide if she wanted him to set something up for her and was picking out a good prospect.

"Do you ever miss it?" she asked, her voice sounding far away.

"Miss what?" He was accustomed to conversational leaps from her, but this one he couldn't follow.

"Football."

"How could I miss it? I live it."

She returned her focus to him, gazing earnestly into his eyes. "No, not just hanging around the locker room and the practice field and reporting about football. I mean playing, yourself. You could have been one of them," she said, indicating the noisy table full of athletes.

What had brought that on? he wondered. "I doubt if I could have been one of them," he said. "I don't think I could have been good enough."

"From what I've heard, you were."

"I never set out to make a career out of sports. I always wanted to be a writer. That was what was important to me." He shrugged. "Sports just gave me an opportunity to make a living as a writer."

"Oh." She nodded, then looked down at the table and concentrated on her food.

He watched her, noticing the slight flush on her cheeks that probably had little to do with the heat of the food. She still wasn't meeting his eyes. She had actually been concerned about him, he realized. She had cared. "Maddy," he said, but she continued to avoid eye contact. He reached across the table to capture her left hand where it rested on the table. "Maddy, thanks."

"For what?" she asked, a little too breezily.

"For caring. Most people just try to avoid the subject, so everyone has gone around for years thinking I've suffered some devastating loss and feeling sorry for me. Thanks for letting me set the record straight."

She looked back up at him and smiled. "I guess I shouldn't have spent so much time calling you a dumb, washed-up jock."

Since they were getting so personal, he decided to ask some questions of his own. "What about you? You're in Dallas reporting on nightclubs and how to find a mate, but you used to talk about wanting to report from international hot spots. Do you have any regrets?"

She winced and broke eye contact as she shoved food around her plate with her fork. His question had apparently struck more of a nerve than hers had. "I don't know," she finally said, her voice not much more than a whisper that he had to struggle to hear over the music from the loudspeaker. "I don't really know if that was ever what I really wanted, or if it was just what I thought I wanted. It seemed like the right thing to say at the time, even though I usually enjoyed reading the entertainment pages more. I just wish sometimes that I had at least tried so I could have known if that was what I wanted to do."

"So it hurts a bit when I tease you about it."

She looked back up at him. "Yes, it does."

"I'm sorry. I won't do it anymore."

A smile tugged at the corners of her mouth. "Do you promise?"

"Scout's honor. That is, unless you make me mad by calling me a dumb jock."

Now she was really smiling. "Okay, so we're even. We now know how much we've been irritating each other all these years." She raised her glass, and he brought his up to face hers. "Here's to a new start on a friendship where we try not to annoy each other." She clinked her glass against his and they both took a sip.

"That's what I'd tell the guys in the locker room," he said.

"What?"

"That you're my friend."

She pondered that for a moment, then said, "I can deal with that. But if any of those hunks are interested, I might be available," she added with a sly grin.

He wasn't sure he liked the idea, and he didn't intend to bring up the option if the subject came up in the locker room. "I'll see what I can do for you," he said. "But you can't write about it if it works unless it's part of the book."

"I think that's the last chapter, so wait until then."

They finished their meal, and Derek paid the check. They walked back to the truck side by side, close, but not quite touching. Even so, Derek was aware of Maddy's proximity. When had this happened? he wondered. He just wished he knew what to do next. When they reached the truck, he opened the door for her and helped her up into the cab. Then he jogged around the truck to reach his side. When he climbed into his seat, she already had her window rolled down. Her baseball cap shadowed her face from the ghostly parking lot lights so he couldn't read her expression.

He started the engine, bringing the radio to life in the middle of the Righteous Brothers' "Unchained Melody." With a gasp of delight, Maddy reached to turn the radio up. Apparently forgetting his presence, she sang along with the radio, slightly out of tune but with great emotion. He remained silent, letting her have her moment. There was a certain alchemy at work, with the starry sky, the night breeze, a romantic song on the radio and the unguarded enthusiasm of the woman next to him. He wondered how long he could keep driving before he had to take her home.

The song ended, and Maddy sank back against the seat with a satisfied sigh. "I just love that song," she breathed.

"I noticed." He refrained from commenting on her singing. That would be sure to spoil the mood.

"This has been nice," she said after a few moments of silence. "Thanks for dinner. I'll have to remember that place."

"Yeah, it's a good one for Tex-Mex," Derek replied, cursing himself for not being able to come up with anything better than small talk. If he couldn't make a decent conversation with someone he'd known for years, how could he expect to do well trying to get to know a stranger?

It seemed an eternity—or perhaps just a moment—before Derek parked in front of Maddy's apartment building. She picked up her camera bag and started to open her door. "Thanks again for dinner. This was fun," she said as she got out.

He hurried to unbuckle his seat belt and get out of the truck. "Wait a second," he said. "In this neighborhood, I'd better walk you to your door."

"I walk myself to my door all the time," she said, then she paused to wait for him. "But I will let you play knight in shining armor for me this time."

He caught up with her, and she slipped an arm around his waist and gave it a squeeze. "You're so sweet," she said. He didn't say anything, just put his arm around her shoulders. They walked like that to her door.

There they paused again. Derek didn't want to just walk away. "I guess we found that the class idea could be effective," he said. "But what are you going to write about this?"

"We don't have to mention that we already knew the person we met."

"And we'd better leave out a few more details, or it will give it all away."

She smiled. "But it will be nice to have some success to report, for a change."

He didn't reply. He couldn't take his eyes off her smiling lips. He could hear his heartbeat, so loud he was sure the whole neighborhood could hear it. Gravity seemed to be pulling him forward, closer and closer to Maddy. As if in anticipation, she tilted her head back and closed her eyes.

It took almost no effort for him to lean forward and kiss her. In fact, it would have taken more effort not to do so. At first, he just gently brushed her lips with his. But when she opened her lips against his and wrapped her arms around his waist to bring him closer, he dropped all pretense at anything resembling a friendly, brotherly kiss.

This kiss contained more raw passion than he had been aware he felt for her, and her response was even more surprising. She gave a soft groan from the back of her throat as she teased his lips with her tongue and molded her body against his. With a groan of his own, he tightened his hold on her and trailed kisses from her lips, down her cheek and behind her ear.

Then sanity returned, and he pulled back. She didn't release him completely, remaining instead within the circle of his arms and resting her head against his shoulder. "Oh, my," she breathed. "Who saw that one coming?"

"That was not on the agenda when I left home this morning. None of this was," he assured her.

She stopped him from apologizing by placing a finger against his lips. "There's something to be said for spontaneity," she said with a smile.

"Let's avoid mentioning this in the paper, if you don't mind," he said, fighting to bring his breathing back to normal.

"I agree, if only to keep Rhona from catching wind of this. I'd never hear the end of it."

"And we have an assignment to complete. What do we have to do next?"

"I can't think of it right now. I'll give you a call in the morning."

He grinned. "I thought I was supposed to be the one to say I'll call you."

She shrugged, but he could see her smile even in the dim light. "Okay, if that's the way you want it. You call me."

He waited until she was safely inside, with the door shut and locked behind her, before he turned and walked down the sidewalk to his truck. When he started the engine, the oldies station came on. He started to switch back to his favorite country station, then changed his mind. Maybe they'd play that Righteous Brothers song again.

*Hers:*

Taking a fun class has to be the best suggestion I've found so far in this book. I am pleased to report that I did meet someone interesting, and I even had a date. The concept behind the suggestion does make sense: it's a good way to meet people with whom you have something in common. But the value of the concept goes beyond that.

To begin with, if you choose something you really enjoy, you'll still walk away from the experience having learned something worthwhile, even if you don't meet someone, so you won't have wasted your time, no matter what happens. If you do see someone interesting, you automatically have a topic for conversation and don't have to rely on boring small talk. Sometimes the class you choose automatically leads to opportunities to get to know a classmate better. My class entailed an out-of-class assignment that was best done with a partner.

My partner and I met to work on our assignment,

and the homework led to dinner and a nice good-night kiss. Try this one. It's fun.

*His:*

For those of you who've come to the conclusion that I'm some kind of loser, I'm not. I have now actually had a date, which I suppose means this tactic will work for just about anyone.

I don't know that I can give all the credit to the book, though. True, it was this advice that put me in the situation. But once there, I still could have missed meeting this woman simply because before that evening I didn't open my eyes to see what was before me. It's enough to make me want to go back and try all the earlier suggestions again. Who knows what I might have missed because I wasn't looking for the right thing?

I'm beginning to think this book needs a sequel on following through. The suggestions in this book only put you in the situation where you might meet someone—you still have to put forth some effort to actually build a relationship. One thing I've learned so far is that Miss Right isn't going to drop from the sky into my lap without me having to make any effort.

# 9

Maddy could feel all eyes in the newsroom watching her as she read the columns posted on the bulletin board under the heading, Our Mystery Lovers. Next to the mounted columns was a posting of the newsroom pool about the identities of the "mystery lovers." She noticed that her name showed up in several of the predictions. Derek's was nowhere on the list. For that, she breathed a little sigh of relief. No one had yet guessed the truth. She didn't even want to think about newsroom reaction when their identities were revealed.

She knew she hadn't dropped any clues in her column about what had actually happened on Saturday night, but she reread Derek's column to see if he had given anything away. As she read, the tiny hairs at the nape of her neck stood on end, and goose bumps rippled the skin on her arms. She hated to read too much between the lines, but it almost sounded like the evening had been really meaningful for him. She didn't even want to think about what it had meant to her.

Realizing she'd spent far too much time at the bulletin board to look casual, she made her way to her desk. She was relieved to notice that, contrary to her paranoid delusions, no one in the newsroom seemed to be paying the least bit of attention to her. Dropping her knapsack on her desk, she sank into her chair. Despite the lack of scrutiny, she still had that creepy feeling of her nerves standing on end and her stomach churning.

When she started the *Finding the Perfect Mate* project, she'd had no intention of forming a deep, lasting relationship. She just hoped to get through the assignment without making a complete fool of herself. When she made the bet with Derek, she just wanted enough success to win. The last thing she expected was to find herself becoming involved with her partner, or to have him falling for her.

It was just his natural shyness, she told herself. It was easier for him to try to develop a relationship with her than to meet anyone new. She was simply the most comfortable target for him. And Saturday had been so perfect and so emotionally charged that any couple would have ended the evening the same way they had. That didn't mean it meant anything at all.

She knew him well enough to know that he would carry through with his promise to call her, so she knew she'd better have the information on the next step in their assignment. She pulled the book from her knapsack and flipped to the next-to-last chapter.

*Initially, sports and romance don't seem to make the ideal combination, but think about it. You have pounding hearts, sweaty bodies and heightened emotions, which make romance a natural side effect.*

*If you play a sport, find a place where there will be a lot of people and play ball! You don't have to be professional-caliber. Sometimes, in fact, it can be very helpful to be a novice. You'll find that experts are more than willing to provide a few pointers, especially to someone they find attractive!*

*Participation in team sports (coed, of course!) is a*

*good way to meet people. The automatic bonding of a*
*team makes it even easier to bond romantically.*

*If sports are completely beyond your abilities, spec-*
*tator events will do. Here you'll also find camaraderie*
*with other fans, plus the intensity of emotion that*
*makes everyone more attractive.*

"I think I'm going to gag," Maddy muttered to herself. The
author's breathless exuberance was beginning to get on her
nerves. She also found the big-game-hunting attitude toward meeting people offensive. More than ever, she looked
forward to ending the assignment.

But now she had to come up with a sport. She was the
most nonathletic person she knew, unless it was possible to
count dancing as a sport. Her friends had always been so
amazed that someone so completely lacking in coordina-
tion in any athletic endeavor could manage intricate dance
steps in rhythm to the music. She wasn't even interested in
watching sports. As far as she was concerned, professional
sports were simply an excuse for grown men to act like children and be paid obscene sums of money to do so. She had
gone to a couple of football games in high school and college, and that was the extent of her athletic involvement.

She didn't even know where to start on this tactic. If she
tried participating, she would only make herself a laugh-
ing-stock. If she tried being a spectator, she would only ex-
pose her ignorance. Maybe she could ask Derek to set her up
with one of those football players he knew, but that
wouldn't really be using athletics. That would be a setup by
friends, which was the next chapter. Derek probably
wouldn't be too thrilled by that idea, either.

Her desk phone rang and she fumbled for it, shoving
aside a pile of news releases she needed to file. "Life-styles.
This is Madeline," she answered.

"Madeline?" a deep, sexy voice came through the receiver. "I'm sorry, I must have the wrong number. I was looking for the Mad Hatter."

The voice wasn't anything she had heard before, but there was no mistaking that nickname. It had to be Derek. Despite the flutter the voice caused in the pit of her stomach, she played along with the joke. "Oh, well, there's no Mad Hatter here. I was having a good hair day, so I'm bareheaded today."

"In that case, let's forget the conversation. I have to see this in person. I'll be there as soon as I can."

"You've seen me without a hat before," she reminded him, keeping her voice low and glancing around the newsroom to make sure her conversation wasn't overheard.

"Oh, yeah, I have. You do have hair, don't you?"

Her anxiety about him eased somewhat at his willingness to joke. After reading his column, she had been worried that he would be spouting poetic declarations of love. This would have been just too weird. Jokes she could deal with. "Yes, I have hair. And you must be on the endangered species list."

"Why do you say that?"

"You said you would call, and you did."

"But you have something I want."

"Oh, come on. You can't be innocent. How often does a man call when he says he's going to?"

"I always do."

Shaking her head and smiling, although she knew he couldn't see her, she said, "Then you really are a jewel. I'm glad you called."

"But you have something I want."

She twirled the phone cord around her finger. "Really? What might that be?"

"Our next assignment."

"You're just no fun. You know what they say about all work and no play. But I think you'll like this one. It's right up your alley. In fact, I bet you can get a date on this one without having to resort to hitting on someone you already know."

If he caught her pointed dig, his voice didn't betray him. "And what might my lucky assignment be? The suspense is killing me."

"Sports."

"Sports are romantic?"

She read from the book, "Pounding hearts, sweaty bodies and heightened emotions."

"I don't know that romance is the right word for that. What does it say to do about sports?"

"Get around people and participate in a sport. It's pretty simple."

"You're right, that should be easy. In fact, I just agreed to fill in for a friend of mine on his softball team while he's on vacation. That should work. If you like, you could probably get on the team, too. They always need women on coed teams."

Was he trying to arrange it so she'd be the one he "met" again? She didn't want to take any chances. "Sorry, but I don't do anything that involves spherical objects being hurled in my general direction. I'll find something else to do."

"Okay, suit yourself. But I have a feeling I may pull ahead on our bet on this one."

"We'll see. I can't wait to read your next column." And she hoped that anything romantic in it wasn't about her. She liked Derek, and he would make a wonderful husband for somebody someday, but not her. His sexy body and easygoing good nature were nice, but they couldn't make up for their total lack of anything in common, except for a vague interest in taking pictures of nature. She didn't want to spend an entire relationship traipsing through wilderness with a camera slung around her neck.

"Have you had your pictures developed yet?" he asked, as if he were reading her mind. "If you want, we could get together before the class Friday night and pick the best ones."

"I'll let you know when I get mine back. I'm not sure I want them displayed in public."

"Okay," he said. She thought she detected a touch of disappointment in his voice, but she could be imagining things. "Well, I guess I'll talk to you later. Give me a call if you want to compare photos."

"I will," she promised. She hung up the phone, feeling a bit guilty. He probably had written the column just to make it sound more like a meaningful date than the rare case of overexcited hormones between friends that it had been. He hadn't meant anything by it, and he wasn't trying to finagle another date. He was just being nice, like he always was, which was one of the reasons she liked him. Now that he had quit teasing her about being a foreign correspondent, he was even nicer. If only she could break him of calling her "Mad Hatter," she'd really be happy.

But if he was so perfect, why was she terrified that he wanted her, or worse, that she wanted him? She didn't want to think about that now.

She put her concerns behind her and went to work on the preview of the next night's concert. She had interviewed the band by phone from their previous stop, and now all she had to do was write the fill-in-the-blanks, "We're glad to be in whatever city this is; we're trying something new with this album" story. Bosnia was beginning to look much more interesting, even if it was a little more dangerous. If she got caught in the mosh pit at this concert, though, Bosnia might seem safe in comparison.

Derek checked out the lineup in the dugout as he braced his bat across his shoulders and twisted back and forth to loosen his back. Softball had never been his best sport, but it was relatively easy on his bad knee, as long as he was careful. Playing in a neighborhood league like this one should be no trouble.

A couple of the other players played catch, tossing the ball back and forth to each other. He recognized the first baseman—or woman, as was the case. As he recalled, her name was Linda. She was tall, with an athletic build, but she still moved with an easy grace. Watching her throw a softball was like watching poetry in motion, with perfect form and no wasted movement. She was efficient and elegant at the same time.

But he was probably getting ahead of himself. He didn't even know for sure if she was single. It was hard to tell on the softball diamond because she wore a glove on her left hand, and she would probably take off any good jewelry before playing. He'd have to be careful here. He wondered if the book's author had thought about the possibility of a ball glove hiding a wedding ring. Probably not. From what he'd read, the closest the author came to sports was probably throwing an elegant Super Bowl party without even knowing who was playing.

The warm-up period ended, and it was time for the game to begin. Derek's team was first at bat. He took a seat in the dugout and was pleasantly surprised when Linda sat next to him. "You're the new guy, aren't you?" she asked.

It wasn't the most eloquent of conversational openers, but it was better than anything he'd come up with. "Yeah, I'm filling in for Randy while he's on vacation."

"Good. I hope you know what you're doing."

That wasn't reassuring. As his turn to bat drew nearer and nearer, he hoped he didn't make a complete fool of himself. It had been a long time since he'd played either softball or baseball. When it was his turn on deck, he swung his bat back and forth and wished he could get rid of the butterflies in his stomach. He hadn't been this nervous since the first time he stepped on the field at Memorial Stadium as a Texas Longhorn, and that time it had been due more to excitement than true nerves.

Fortunately, this was slow-pitch softball. When he stepped into the batter's box and saw the ball coming toward him, he knew he could hit it if it came near the plate. For the first two pitches, it didn't. The pitcher proved the amateur quality of the teams, and he relaxed a little bit. On the third pitch, he swung and connected with the ball with a satisfying thwack, sending it sailing over the field. He dropped his bat and ran for first base, the sound of his team cheering ringing in his ears.

He made it all the way to second base before the fielders came up with the ball and threw it back to the pitcher. Linda was next at bat, and she approached the plate with a confident swagger. She didn't waste any time swinging at the first pitch and sending it straight back at the pitcher, who instinctively ducked. Derek ran on to third base, then looked to see where the ball was. The outfielders were still running in circles, so he ran on home. Linda made it as far as third base.

The next batter made it to first base, which gave Linda the opportunity to run for home. Derek waited for her at the entrance to the dugout to give her a high-five. She returned his congratulations, gave him a measuring look and said, "You're okay."

"Just okay?" His own boldness amazed him. He had never considered himself a very good flirt, unless he was flirting with someone he wasn't trying to attract, like Maddy. Or like Maddy up until a few weeks ago, to be more accurate. He forced Maddy's image out of his mind to concentrate on the woman he was with. Why was this starting to make him feel cheap?

"Let's see how good you are in the field." She tossed her blond French braid over her shoulder and headed to the water jug.

He took off his cap and wiped the sweat from his forehead with the back of his hand, then took a seat on the end of the bench. His team scored one more run before they made their third out and it was time to take the field. Derek played right field, not necessarily a hot spot for action, but it gave him a good view of Linda as she played first base.

She played with the same efficiency and elegance she had shown during warm-ups, but Derek forced himself to keep his mind on the game. That was difficult because he didn't have much to do. The other team's batters weren't very strong, and Linda snagged anything they sent in his direction. Before he had a chance to get his bearings in the field, he was jogging back to the bench.

The remaining innings went pretty much the same way, with Derek's team scoring a few runs, then the other team making their three outs quickly. Derek got on base three more times, scored two runs, struck out twice and was walked during the rest of his at-bats. Linda was the star player, scoring three runs of her own and bringing in five other players.

The team gathered in celebration in front of their dugout and exchanged high-fives. Derek was in the process of congratulating another player when a swat on his rear end made him jump. "What the..." he muttered. That had to be what was known as a low-five. He whirled to see Linda winking at him.

"Good game, slugger," she said. "Any ideas for celebrating?"

"I think the team's going for pizza," he said, realizing even as the words left his mouth that he was risking sounding very foolish. She knew very well what the team had planned. "Unless you had other plans."

"I don't think I'm in the mood for pizza."

"Oh?" He really would prefer going out with the rest of the group, but he was supposedly here to meet women.

"Yeah, I think I'd rather have a burger."

*What the heck,* he thought to himself. "Well, would you like to join me for burgers?"

"I'd love to," she said, latching on to his arm.

A couple of hours later, Derek wished he had gone for pizza. They had gone to a build-your-own-burger kind of place, what Maddy would have referred to as a "yuppie burger fern bar." That was the trouble: he couldn't keep himself from thinking of everything in terms of Maddy. Either he was comparing everything about Linda to Maddy or he was trying to think of what Maddy would say about what was happening. He even thought of what he would tell Maddy about this evening, and he imagined her reaction. The girl was on his brain like one of her crazy hats on her head.

For the hundredth time, he dragged his attention back to Linda, who was reliving her glory days as a college athlete. "You know," she said, gesturing with a french fry, "if I'd been male, I'd be making a million by now, but there isn't much call for a professional women's volleyball player, now is there? Unless I wanted to play some kind of beach circuit where I'm expected to play in a bikini, I was stuck. I had to get a real job."

Derek didn't have much patience for self-pity. "I was a college star, and I'm not making much money," he said.

"Star, or walk-on?"

"Quarterback at the University of Texas."

"What happened?"

"I blew out a knee."

"But you would have been rich and famous if that hadn't happened. That's my point. It's not fair." She punctuated her sentence by biting down on her french fry.

Derek took the chance to get a word in edgewise. "It was the best thing that ever happened to me," he said, then took a bite of his burger so he wouldn't have to say anything more for a moment.

Her eyes widened. "Blowing out your knee?" she asked as soon as she had finished chewing. He nodded. "But how?" she asked.

"Because it forced me to pursue my other interests, which with any luck may have a more lasting impact on my life."

She didn't look like she understood. In her world view, the playing field was all that counted. He didn't even bother to mention his novel. She wouldn't understand that unless it was about a football star whose dreams were shattered by a bad knee. She would be amazed that the word *football* didn't appear once in his book.

"So, anyway," she continued, as if the conversation had never taken a detour, "this softball league has been the salvation of my sanity. I'm an office drone eight to five, Monday through Friday, then after hours, I'm my true self."

"Have you ever considered coaching?"

She looked at him like he was crazy. "Coach? Where?"

"They have baseball and softball leagues for kids. You could be a good role model and give the kids someone to look up to while you taught them the game."

She shook her head. "Nope. I only get the thrill from playing."

If he hadn't driven her to the restaurant, Derek would have been tempted to invent an excuse to leave. Unfortunately, he was too gentlemanly to leave a woman stranded at a restaurant. It was a pity, he thought. Linda was certainly attractive, and she did have something in common with him that did play a major role in his life, but otherwise, they might as well have been living on two different planets. They could never find a common ground between them.

It took Linda a while longer to finish her meal because she didn't interrupt her monologue often enough to eat. Derek endured it all by smiling and nodding at what he hoped were appropriate places. Mentally, he wrote his column on the subject.

Finally she finished her burger and fries and they left. As they walked back to his truck, she swatted his behind again. "We'll tear 'em up Saturday night, won't we, slugger?" she said.

He agreed with her, hoping all the while that Randy would cut his vacation short. The book told him everything he needed to know about meeting women. It didn't say anything about getting rid of them.


Thursday afternoon, Derek put the finishing touches on his story on the newest assistant coach to join the team and sent it by modem to the newspaper. Then he leaned back in his desk chair and stretched his shoulders. He exercised frequently, but the softball game the other night had left him stiff and a bit sore. The soreness was probably more due to tension about hoping he didn't mess up too badly than to an activity related to the game itself.

He glanced at the clock over his desk in his home office. It was still early afternoon, so Maddy should be at her desk working, but not on such a tight deadline that she wouldn't have time to talk. He picked up the phone and dialed.

She answered on the second ring, and this time he didn't go through his tired Mad Hatter routine. That was a last resort for when he couldn't think of anything else to say to her to break the ice. "Hey, Maddy, it's me," he said. "Do you have any pictures you're willing to show in public?"

"Pictures? Oh, yeah, from last weekend. They aren't too bad, I guess."

"Well, do you want to get together before the class to go over what we've got? How about dinner tonight?"

There was a long pause at the other end of the line. "Sorry, I can't tonight. I have plans."

He wondered what kind of plans she meant, but he didn't think he would score any points with her by asking. "Okay, how about tomorrow night before class? I'm doing afternoon drive tomorrow, but I get off the air at six. Class is at eight, so I don't know that we'll have time for anything fancy. But we can grab a quick bite then go to class together—so you don't have to stress your car any more than you have to."

After another long pause she said, "I think you'd just better get something to eat on the way over. You can eat at my place while we look at pictures, if you like." Then she added, "I would like a ride, though. Thanks for offering." He hadn't been aware of the tension in her voice until it eased with her last statement. The contrast was startling.

"Maddy, what's wrong?" he asked.

"Wrong?"

"You sound tense. Are you okay?"

"I'm fine. It's just deadlines, you know."

He didn't think that was it, but he figured she didn't want to talk about it right now. "Then I'd better let you go. I'll see you tomorrow night. Oh, yeah, and have you found a sport yet?"

"I'm still working on it. See you tomorrow." Before he could say anything more, she hung up.

He replaced the receiver in its cradle but continued to stare at it. He had a feeling deadlines were her last worry right now, and he had a feeling he was part of the problem. Kissing her had been a mistake. She may have seemed to enjoy it at the time, but she was probably having second thoughts now. The kiss had shaken the stability of their friendship, just as they had managed to solidify it. Now the lines had blurred and he wasn't sure what he felt about her. All he knew was that he couldn't wait to see her again, and they had to have a talk to get things back on track.

Maddy fluffed the cushions on her futon one more time and surveyed her apartment. It was disgustingly small and shabby and looked like a glorified dorm room, and she felt suddenly ashamed of what she saw. By the time a woman was in her mid-twenties she should have started to build a home, not continue to camp out as if anticipating that her life would change radically at any moment. Hers hadn't changed for several years. She didn't even know what she was waiting for.

The off-key singers selling tires on the radio commercial ended and the show returned. Maddy turned up the volume to hear Derek's voice. "Okay, we're back on 'Sports Talk Live.' I'm Derek Newman and we're on the air with high school standout Mitch Walker. Mitch, you're just a junior in high school, but pro baseball scouts are already making you offers. You're telling them you want to go to college. How do you resist the temptation?''

Maddy couldn't believe she was listening to a radio sports talk show. She had first turned it on in hopes of hearing something she might be able to use for conversation tonight during the ride to class. She hadn't worried about it Saturday, but now she didn't know what direction the conversation would go, and she wanted to be able to steer it away from any analysis of their relationship.

She also had to admit to a bit of curiosity about what Derek did. She read his articles in the paper—or, at least, she had started doing so in the past month or so—but she had the impression that he had a whole other life she didn't know anything about. She was beginning to realize he was more than a former jock using his knowledge of sports to make a living. Not only could he string words together on paper, but he could speak well, with his deep, smooth voice and an eloquence almost equal to his writing.

In a way, she had almost hoped to remind herself why she had nothing much in common with him and no reason to be interested in him, but the radio show captivated her in a way she hadn't been expecting. Most of her apartment was still untidy because she kept finding herself in front of the radio, listening, rather than cleaning. The show was only about sports in the most general way. It was really more about people, and Derek had a talent for bringing the people to life. How could she ever have thought him shy?

The teenage baseball player finished telling about his goals for his life and how they included college. ''But couldn't you accomplish most of those things without going to college first?'' Derek asked. ''After all, you'd be making a lot of money.''

With what Maddy thought was a lot of poise, the boy responded, ''But what if I got hurt that first year and it was all over? If I go to college now, I've got a scholarship, so I can at least get an education and do something with my life. If I'm a high school graduate playing pro baseball and my career ends, no one's going to help me do anything. I saw what happened to you, and I see what you're able to do now because you went to college.''

There was a slight pause, then Derek said, "Mitch, I wish we could play a tape of what you just said to every would-be athlete in school today. Your mind is your most important asset, whether or not you make it in sports. I hope the pros are smart enough to wait on you, because when you get out of college, you won't just be an outstanding athlete, you'll be a smart man. We'll be back with more sports talk after this.''

Once again, Maddy found herself standing in front of the radio. If she wasn't careful, she could get addicted to this. It was so much more enthralling than the parade of transvestites having affairs with their wives' sisters on the television talk shows. She could hardly believe that on what she called the all-testosterone, all the time radio station there was actually a show that didn't glorify on-the-field achievements over everything else. She already knew from the conversation Saturday night that Derek didn't appear to hold any regrets over the loss of his athletic glory days, but if he wasn't careful, he'd start sounding more like a poet than a jock.

After the commercial break, Derek took calls from listeners, most of whom agreed with Mitch's decision. Between the two of them, Mitch and Derek managed to change the opinions of those who disagreed. Many of those seemed to be young men about Mitch's age who thought he should take the money and run, but Mitch and Derek's arguments were too well-thought-out and too well expressed to wither under the fire of opposition.

Maddy was glad when the show went off the air because it meant she might finally get something accomplished. It also meant Derek would be there in half an hour. She had just straightened the place somewhat and changed into leggings and a long, lightweight sweater when he knocked on her door.

She opened the door to see him standing there, wearing jeans, an oxford-cloth shirt and a tweed sportcoat, carrying a take-out bag. It was the first time she'd seen him since she said goodbye to him Saturday night, and she had forgotten just how good he looked. She had to restrain herself from the crazy impulse to repeat the whole scene from Saturday night. Instead, she said, "Oh, hi," and stepped back to allow him inside.

"I don't know if you've had dinner yet, so I picked up sandwiches for both of us," he said, placing the take-out bag on her kitchen countertop. "If you don't want yours, you can save it for later."

"Actually, I haven't eaten," she said. She didn't tell him it was because she'd been frantically cleaning her apartment to prepare it for him while she listened to his show. "Thanks for thinking of me."

He opened the bag and pulled out two soft drinks and two sandwiches. "They're both the same, turkey breast, lettuce, tomato and sprouts on wheat bread. I had a feeling you'd like that."

"Your feeling was right," she said, perching on a bar stool and reaching for a sandwich. "It's my favorite. How did you know?"

"Informed guess," he said, sitting on the stool next to her and taking the other sandwich. "I usually end up eating lunch with you when I'm downtown, and I noticed what you usually order."

"I'm almost impressed that you noticed something like that." She took a bite of her sandwich and chewed, using the activity to avoid having to talk to him for a while. If he didn't stop being so nice to her, she was going to grab him and never let him go, and she wasn't so sure that would be a good idea. They were good friends now, after years of sparring. Why not enjoy that before pushing anything else?

"Speaking of impressed," she said after an uncomfortable lull, "I caught your radio show this afternoon."

He raised an eyebrow. "You did? I didn't know you listened to sports radio."

"I usually don't. I was just scanning the dial, and I heard your voice, so I listened." He didn't have to know that she was scanning the dial for the purpose of finding his show because she didn't know what station it was on. "Anyway, I was really impressed."

"Yeah, that Mitch is something special, isn't he? I'm thinking of trying to freelance a piece on him to some national magazine. He's such an outstanding role model."

"I wasn't talking about Mitch. I was talking about you. You had to find him, recognize what he was and bring that out of him on the show. I was impressed with you. Is your show always like that?"

He was flushing from the collar of his shirt to the roots of his blond hair. Maybe she'd laid the compliments on a bit thick, but she had meant every word. "It's not always that inspiring, but yes, I do try to stick to the theme of the people behind the scores. You can hear sports scores all over town, but I think I've got something different."

"I really underestimated you," she said, then hurried to take another bite so she wouldn't be expected to talk to him again for a while. She had said far too much already. Fortunately, he was astute enough not to push further, and he wasn't the type to try mining for compliments. All the more reason why he would drive her crazy if she had to be around him much more.

They finished their sandwiches in silence, then she jumped up before the conversation could begin again and got her packet of photographs. ''I think I got some pretty good ones. At least, I'm not embarrassed to show them in public.''

He bent over her shoulder to look at her pictures. She could feel his warm breath on her neck, and she had to focus all her energy on the photographs to keep herself from molding her body against his once more and kissing him senseless. It had been bad enough when she started actually liking him rather than finding him irritating. Now she had to go and develop a powerful physical attraction for him. They had to get through only one more chapter of the book before they finished the assignment, she reminded herself.

''I like the way the one with the ducklings came out,'' he said.

''What?'' His voice startled her back to reality. ''Oh yeah, that's one of my favorites,'' she said, recovering her wits. ''Let's see yours.''

Derek took an envelope from his jacket pocket and pulled out the photographs. She flipped through them, whistling in amazement at the way he had captured motion on film. ''The one with the jackrabbit is incredible,'' she said. ''He looks like he's about to leap off the picture.''

''Thanks. I don't think either of us is going to look bad tonight.'' He glanced at his watch, then said, ''Speaking of which, we'd better get going.''

Maddy collected her purse and let him lead the way to the truck. When he started the engine, she was amazed to find that the radio was still tuned to the oldies station. Had he been listening to it all the time, or had he just changed it for her? She hoped they didn't play any truly romantic songs. If they played "Unchained Melody" she'd be undone.

Fortunately, they were doing a "Friday Night Sock Hop," with plenty of fast songs for dancing—nothing to make her start having crazy thoughts about Derek again. All she had to do was make it through this evening, then she would find herself some sports-related activity and meet a man so incredible he'd make her forget all about Derek. She'd have a number of dates with him so she'd win the bet, then she'd have Derek at her beck and call for a week. With a groan she slid down in her seat. She couldn't win. No matter what she did, she'd be stuck with him.

# 10

Derek wished he could figure out Maddy's problem. She was running hot and cold, and he had no idea which way she would go next. She had been edgy when he first came over, then she had warmed up a bit, then at class she had been distant. Now as he drove her home, she sat beside him but seemed miles away. "What's up, Maddy?" he finally asked. She blinked and turned toward him, looking as if she'd forgotten he was even there.

"Huh?" she said.

"Earth to Maddy. It looks like you're traveling the galaxy without leaving home. What's up?"

She looked away and shrugged her shoulders. "Nothing. I was just thinking."

"That's funny. I didn't smell anything burning."

She shot him a glare, but he felt rewarded to see the faintest hint of a smile tugging at the corners of her mouth. "It wasn't anything that profound," she assured him. "I was just thinking about all the crazy things we've done in the past few weeks."

"I don't know that I'd call it crazy," he said. "Let's see, we've gone dancing, gone grocery shopping, walked the dog, gone to church, helped organize a group to help the homeless and taken a class on nature photography. Are we wild and crazy, or what?"

She laughed and shook her head. "That's not what I meant. I might have done most of those things on my own, but I never would have thought about doing them just to meet men. In fact, I never worried about meeting men. Now it's like I'm obsessed with it. I size up every man I meet and evaluate his potential as 'Mr. Right.' That is crazy."

"Every man?"

"Just about."

"So, how do I stack up?"

"Not you," she amended hastily. "I mean, I work with you. You're not a candidate."

"I'm not?" Derek tried to keep a light tone, but her remark stung. Not that he would have put himself in the running as a candidate to start with, but after that kiss last weekend he would have hoped she might have at least given him a passing thought. "I'm surprised they don't have a chapter in that book about meeting people at work. From what I've seen, there's a lot of that going on, although I don't know what you could do about it, short of changing jobs."

"It's a big mistake to get involved with someone at work. It adds too much tension to the situation."

"Whatever." He didn't feel like arguing with her right now, even though she seemed to be almost baiting him. He turned up the radio so the silence in the truck's cab wouldn't become unbearable.

The oldies radio station had ended their "sock hop" of fast songs and was now playing dreamy slow-dance numbers. It probably wasn't the best background music for the circumstances, but he didn't want to start an argument by changing stations. If she had a problem with it, she could switch.

After a series of commercials, he recognized the opening notes of "Unchained Melody." He remembered how Maddy had reacted to that song the last time they had been out together, and he watched her out of the corner of his eye to see her reaction. This time, though, she didn't sit up straight and sing along. Instead, she slumped wearily against the door and sighed. He sighed, as well. She was running cold again, and since he had no idea why, there was nothing he could do to stop it.

When they reached her apartment, he walked her to the door, but this time he didn't even try to kiss her good-night. If he could read her at all, he was pretty sure she didn't want him to. But he could be wrong, he thought as he pulled out of his parking place and noticed her still standing in the doorway, watching him leave.

Maddy slammed the door behind her as she entered her apartment. She wasn't sure what she was mad about. True, he hadn't kissed her this time, but she could hardly blame him after the way she had treated him. She'd be lucky if he ever spoke to her again.

She also wasn't sure why she had acted that way. She might as well be back in junior high. The problem was, she wasn't clear in her own mind what exactly she wanted from him.

She liked Derek. Of that she was certain. Before the assignment had started, she hadn't been so sure. Now, she liked having him as a friend. It was good to have a male friend to talk to, and she knew this could be a friendship to last beyond the assignment.

But she also liked his kisses. She liked the feel of his body next to hers. She liked the way his eyes crinkled when he smiled and the way he blushed when she complimented him. Part of her longed to be much more than friends.

Their friendship had taken so long to establish that she was afraid to strain it by taking it any further. Maybe that was what was so confusing about all this. It was as good an explanation as any, she thought.

And she could see only one remedy to the problem. She needed to go out there and find herself a man so she wouldn't have to worry about having mixed feelings about Derek.

Unfortunately, this was the sports chapter, and that was easier said than done.

Maddy gave the laces on her skates a firm tug, then tied them in a double bow. She didn't know if ice skating at the mall counted as athletic activity, but it was the best she could manage. True, it would be much more romantic at Christmastime, but in springtime, the rink was less crowded.

She took a few wobbly steps toward the rink, then clung to the railing as she eased her way onto the ice. If she wanted to impress someone ice skating, it would probably work better if she skated more often than once a year, but she didn't have a private rink for practicing. Then again, she thought as she let go of the railing long enough to coast a few feet, if all else failed, she could meet someone by running into him.

She caught the railing again with a sigh of relief, then paused to catch her breath. Looking back across the rink, she realized she'd only made it less than a quarter of the way around. With a deep sigh, she let go of the railing again and took a cautious glide forward. She wobbled a bit, but didn't lose her balance. Another glide forward, and she was beginning to get her "ice legs." She still kept close to the edge, within arm's reach of the railing, but she made a complete circuit of the ice unassisted.

The next time around, she moved farther from the railing. She was still too busy trying to remain upright to look for any potential candidates, but she'd worry about that when she had a little more confidence. She was just feeling almost like a skater when something came out of nowhere to knock her off-balance. She felt herself falling, but a pair of strong arms caught her and held her upright.

"Sorry about that. Are you okay?" She nodded, still shaken and winded. When she looked up, she saw a man on hockey skates whizzing away. He made a quick turn around the ice, weaving expertly around the other skaters. She stayed where she was, watching him. He was fairly tall, though not as tall as Derek—why was she always comparing men to him? But unlike Derek, he was dark-haired and on the slender side. He was also kind of cute.

When he approached her around the corner of the rink, he came to a stop with an impressive snowplow. "Are you okay?" he asked again. "I'm normally in better control of myself, but I was trying to avoid one of those daredevil kids."

"Oh, that's okay. I was probably in your way," she said, giving him a big grin. "I'm not exactly an expert."

"You're doing fine," he assured her. "You look pretty good for a beginner. How many times have you been skating?"

"About ten."

"This year?"

"In my life."

"Oh. In that case, you're doing great." He raised an eyebrow at her and gave her a grin that could make the ice melt. "Care for a turn around the ice?"

This was working out better than she had hoped. "I'd love to." He offered her an arm, which she took. After one gliding step, she found herself clutching his arm desperately. They were moving slowly by his standards, but she felt like she was flying across the ice. Once she became accustomed to the sensation, she started enjoying the feel of cool air rushing off the ice to caress her face and the scraping hiss of her skates on the ice. The warmth from the man next to her wasn't bad, either.

After a couple of turns around the ice, she eased her death grip on his arm. "Thanks, I was beginning to lose feeling there," he said with another one of those melting grins.

"Sorry," she breathed. "I'm not too confident about this skating thing."

"You're doing fine. Not ready to try out for pairs skating at the Olympics, but good enough for a novice."

"Thanks. You're obviously an old pro." She was blatantly stroking the male ego, but she wanted some success on this outing. She was pulling out all the stops.

He glowed under her praise, which diminished him somewhat in her eyes. Derek at least had the grace to be embarrassed. "Oh, I've been skating since I was a kid up north. I used to play hockey, but I quit when the bruises seemed to start hurting more."

"How long ago was that?"

"About six weeks."

"You weren't professional, were you?" She didn't really think he was, but she was still trying to flatter his ego, even if it made her gag to do so.

He laughed. "No, just a casual league, kind of like you have softball around here."

Once again, he managed to remind her of Derek. He had a softball game that evening, at a field near her neighborhood. She shook her head as if to chase the thought away. She was here trying to meet men, and she was hoping to snag this guy, whatever his name was. She didn't need to be thinking about Derek. She had enough to worry about for the moment.

"Let's see if you can make it on your own for a little while," her mystery skater said. "I really think you're getting the hang of this."

Reluctantly, she pried her fingers from around his arm. She felt a bit wobbly at first, then she reminded herself that this was no different than what she had been doing for the last ten minutes or so. Her equilibrium steadied, and she made a tentative stroke across the ice. So far, so good. She began skating, really skating, rather than lurching around. She moved much more slowly than she had with someone to lean on, but better than she had before he had crashed into her. He barely expended any effort keeping up with her.

"Hey, I did it!" she cried out when she had completed a full circuit around the ice. She flashed him a grin that she didn't have to force.

Just then, the rink's disk jockey's voice came over the loudspeaker. "It's time to move in reverse!"

"Oh, no!" Maddy wailed. "I just got used to one direction, and I have no idea how to turn around."

"Here, I can help on that one," her skating partner said. He put his arm around her waist, then skated in a small circle with her as the pivot point. Soon, she was facing the opposite direction.

"Neat trick," she said, fighting a satisfied smile. Things were looking better and better. She really wished she knew his name, but introductions could be awkward at this point. Maybe they could laugh about it later when he asked for her phone number.

He disappointed her by releasing his hold on her waist as soon as she was facing the proper direction. "Let's see how you do now," he said, taking an extra step away from her. Suppressing a sigh, she began skating again. Right now she didn't want a skating lesson, she wanted a man, especially one as cute as this one.

A small child darting among the other skaters inadvertently worked into her scheme by cutting her off and sending her reeling. Her helper rushed to her rescue, preventing her from falling. She clung to him a little more than was really necessary, noting as she did so that he smelled nice. She wasn't sure which exact brand of after-shave lotion he used, but it smelled expensive.

He patted her on the back. "Are you okay?"

She nodded, then gave him a shaky grin. "Yeah, but I think those little demons should be locked up. Do they ever have grown-ups-only skating here?"

"I don't know, but it sounds like a good idea." He gave her a crooked grin that made him look even cuter. "I must confess, though, to having been one of those demon children when I was a kid."

"So I guess there's hope for those brats, after all, huh?"

This time, he maintained his hold on her as they skated. She enjoyed the security, but she would have liked the option of trying more on her own. This could be an indication that he would be smothering in a relationship, she thought, then mentally chastised herself for thinking like that. She was just hoping to get him to ask her out. She didn't have to be analyzing him in terms of being a life's mate. Neither the assignment nor the bet were that serious.

He stayed with her throughout the whole afternoon skating session. Unfortunately, skating was all they did. There was no conversation worth remembering, and she couldn't think of anything to ask without sounding nosy. It was kind of difficult to ask a man personal questions when she didn't even know his name. But, she reminded herself, this was just the opening act. After they were through skating, he could invite her for coffee and then they would get to know each other.

Maddy's legs felt like spaghetti when the buzzer finally blew to end the skating session and clear the ice. She wasn't sure she would remember how to walk. She had already decided she deserved a slice of cheesecake for all the exercise she had done that afternoon. Now all he had to do was invite her for coffee and dessert.

She stumbled on wobbly legs to her locker, where she retrieved her shoes. Then she collapsed on a bench to change out of her skates. He sat next to her. This was looking really good, she thought. He went with her as she turned in her skates, then they walked side by side to the exit. There they paused.

She looked up at him expectantly, her heart racing in anticipation. "This has been fun," he said.

"Yes, it has," she agreed. "Now that I'm not making a fool of myself, I'll have to do it more often. Thanks for your help."

"No problem," he said. "Well, good luck." And with that, he turned and walked away, his skates slung over his shoulder.

She was too stunned to react at all. When he was out of sight, she thought of all the things she should have done, like introduce herself, invite him for coffee or suggest they meet again. She thought she'd been flirting enough for him to get the message, but he must have been more dense than the average man, or else not interested.

That possibility was too depressing to even contemplate. Instead, she went to the bakery in the food court and ordered a slice of cherry cheesecake and a cappuccino. She wasn't so sure she wanted him, anyway. After all, if she kept thinking of Derek when she was with him, that meant that what's-his-name couldn't be worth much as a man. She was better off without him, she decided as she let a rich bite of cheesecake melt in her mouth.

Besides, she still had one more shot with this tactic. The book had said you could meet people at an athletic event without having to participate. Derek had a game that evening, and he had said something about single men on his team. She might just swing by the field. Watching well-toned, sweaty bodies had to be more fun than skating with a dweeb, anyway.

From her perch on the top row of the battered aluminum bleachers, Maddy decided that while "sweaty" was an appropriate adjective for this group, "well-toned" was not. Most of the players looked like armchair athletes whose primary motivation for playing had to be the post-game beer. The exceptions were Derek and the woman playing first base. In close-fitting uniform shorts, Derek proved to have an even better body than she had thought. He really was solid muscle.

The uniform also showed off to full advantage the body of the woman at first base. It was rather convenient how Derek managed to be playing behind her so that he got a good view of her tight derriere. It would be a miracle if he managed to catch a single ball during the game.

So far, he hadn't seemed to have noticed that Maddy was there. That was fine with her. She had the chance to scope out the men on the field, then at halftime—or whenever they took a break during softball—she could finagle an introduction.

Unfortunately, she wasn't really all that impressed with anyone on either team. Her eyes kept straying back to Derek. It was funny how she so seldom noticed how good-looking he was. She was so used to him that she never thought about it. Now that she tried to survey the field with impartial eyes, she had to admit he was the most handsome man in sight.

A fact the first basewoman seemed to have noticed, as well. She managed to glance over her shoulder at him between each pitch, and she stayed close to him in the dugout when their team was at bat. Maddy noticed with satisfaction that he didn't seem to be paying that much attention to his teammate. It wasn't jealousy, she told herself. She didn't want him. She just didn't want him to win the bet.

Now Derek's team was at bat, and Derek was up next. She noticed the flexing of his shoulder muscles as he swung his bat back and forth. He probably hadn't been joking when he had told her he worked out regularly. It had to be true for him to have a body like that. He swung at the first pitch, and the bat connected with the ball with a loud crack.

"All right, Derek!" she shouted, rising to her feet. "Run!" He made it safely to first base, and while the next batter was coming up to the plate, Derek looked up at the bleachers. Now he knew she was there. Even at that distance, they made eye contact. She thought she saw him wink at her, then he returned his attention to the game.

The next batter also hit the ball, sending it to the middle of the field. Derek dashed toward the next base, but the ball was on its way there, too. He slid into the base, and the umpire ruled him safe. Maddy cheered, but the cheer soon died in her throat. Derek wasn't getting up. Instead, he still lay on the ground, clutching his knee.

# 11

---◆---

*Oh, no,* Maddy thought in dismay, *his bad knee.* With a strangled gasp, she clambered down the bleachers and ran to the field where he lay, surrounded by his teammates. Her heart pounding in her chest, she forced her way through the group and knelt at his side. "Do you have a medic around?" she asked the other players. They all shrugged and went back to their positions, the first basewoman with a muttered comment about weekend warriors trying to act big.

Derek's face was white with pain and his teeth were clenched. "Derek, I think we'd better get you off the field or they're going to run right over you," she said, trying not to let him see her concern.

"Yeah, so much for the fallen hero," he said with a weak smile.

"Do you think you can walk?"

"How good are you at pretending to be a crutch?"

"I guess we'll have to find out." She helped him sit up, then she draped one of his arms across her shoulders and used her legs to lift them both. He got his good leg under him to lift the rest of the way. Then they made it slowly to the edge of the field, with him leaning heavily against her every time he stepped on his right leg. A mild smattering of applause acknowledged his exit. She eased him onto the bottom seat of the bleachers. The game had already resumed before he was seated.

"Do we need to get you to a doctor?" she asked.

He shook his head. "No need. This happens every so often, whenever I get too full of myself and try to play super jock again. It's just a trick knee that goes out on me from time to time. That's why I had to quit playing football." He grimaced, then added, "And it looks like I'll have to cross softball off my list, too. Anyway, I just need to rest, put some ice on it, put it up and it should be fine tomorrow."

"It's your right leg," she noted. "Can you drive?"

He groaned. "I forgot about that. I might be able to make it."

She shook her head. "Don't even try. I'll drive you home. You'll just have to tell me how to get there."

"Maddy, I appreciate the offer, but there's no way I'm going to be able to get this leg in your Bug without extreme pain."

"We'll have to take your truck, anyway. I rode my bike tonight. I don't even have my car here. But that's okay, I'm sure I can handle your truck."

His eyes widened, giving him the look of a rabbit caught in oncoming headlights. "I don't know, Maddy...."

"Come on, Derek. I know your pickup truck is close to sacred, but I don't think you're up to walking home right now."

He sighed. "You're right. I'm just being stupid. Thanks for offering to help."

She squeezed his shoulder. "That's okay. I don't expect you to be at your best right now."

A cheer rose from the crowd, and Derek and Maddy turned to watch the first basewoman sprinting for home plate. She crossed the plate well ahead of the ball, then shot Maddy a glare as she trotted toward the dugout.

"What was that about?" Maddy asked.

Derek shifted his leg using his hands, then leaned back with a groan. "She probably thinks I'm two-timing."

"Why would she think that?"

"I took her to dinner after our last game."

"Oh. I'm sorry," Maddy lamented, remembering why both of them were there. "I shouldn't have come. Now I've messed up your chance to work something out."

"I wasn't going to ask her out again."

The relief that flooded through her alarmed Maddy. "You weren't?" she asked breathlessly.

He shook his head. "I don't think I could stand another evening listening to tales of her athletic prowess." He made a face. "And I hate it when people pat me on the butt."

"I'll have to keep that in mind." It was an intriguing thought, but for now, she had an injured man to take care of. "Ready to go?"

"Let's give it a try," he answered.

Once again, Maddy got her shoulders under Derek's arm and helped him rise. He was more steady now and didn't lean on her as heavily. They moved slowly toward his truck. When they reached the place he had parked, he leaned against the side of the truck and fished his keys out of his pocket. Maddy opened the door and helped him up into the cab.

"Hang on a second," she then said. "I'll go get my bicycle and throw it in the back. Otherwise, I doubt it will be here later." She dashed to where she had chained her bike to the back of the bleachers, unlocked it and wheeled it to Derek's truck, where she lowered the tailgate and shoved it in, taking care not to scrape the paint in the truck's bed too badly. Then she ran around the truck and found that Derek had already unlocked her door.

Once she had settled into the seat, she had to move it forward several inches so she could reach the accelerator. Derek handed her the keys, and she started the engine. "Okay, let's see if I can handle this monster," she said. At his look of alarm, she hurried to add, "Just kidding. I'm sure I can handle it. After all, I can drive a stick shift."

"This is an automatic."

She wrinkled her nose. "I know. You should get a real transmission. Automatics are for wimps."

He leaned his head back against the seat. "We can argue about it later."

"Sorry," she said, and moved the gearshift from Park to Drive. "And don't worry," she said. "I've driven pickup trucks before. Now, where are we going?"

"Do you know where Valley Ranch is?"

"Out there somewhere," she said with a wave of her hand. "I don't usually get that far from downtown."

"Just get on the freeway and go north. I'll let you know when it's time to make the next move."

"The freeway, huh?" She eased out onto the street, heading west toward the freeway. It had been a long time since she'd driven on a highway. Her car couldn't get up to road speed. She didn't admit that to Derek, though. She was confident that she could handle it, and she didn't want to alarm him. He was already clutching the armrest in the door so hard his knuckles were turning white. She hoped it was due more to his pain than to his worry about her driving his truck.

She merged onto the freeway and was grateful for the light Saturday-evening traffic. "Okay, now what?" she asked, glancing over at Derek.

His eyes were closed, but when she spoke, his eyelids fluttered open. "Go west on L.B.J." He inhaled sharply through clenched teeth, moved his leg into a new position with his hands, then closed his eyes again and leaned his head against the window.

Maddy bit her lip and tried to keep her attention on the road. He was really hurting. "I'll have you home soon, don't worry," she reassured him. The situation made her a bit uncomfortable. She wasn't used to being in a position where someone was relying on her. But she was handling herself pretty well, if she said so herself.

She saw her exit up ahead and steered onto the ramp. "Now what?" she asked.

"Take the third exit and go north."

"Okay." She passed the first exit, then asked, "How am I doing so far?"

"What?"

"Driving your truck. How am I handling it?"

His lips twitched into a semblance of his usual smile. "You're doing fine."

"It is kind of different looking down on everything, but I guess you're used to that."

"Is that some kind of remark about my height?" He must be feeling better if he was cracking jokes, she thought.

"If the shoe fits . . ." she shot back. She glanced up to see an exit sign. "Is this it?"

"No, it's the next one."

"I hope you don't have a third-floor apartment."

"No, I'm on the ground floor."

"Good, because I can't carry you."

She moved into the right lane, then took the next exit. At the light, she turned right. "Now, let me know where to go."

He directed her to his apartment complex and to his building. She put the parking brake on, then opened her door and jumped down to the ground. Derek had already opened his door by the time she got around to him. "Wait a second," she warned him. "You don't want to hurt yourself any worse."

"Maddy, it's no big deal. I'll be okay."

"Yeah, sure." She helped him to the door, and she had to admit that he was leaning less heavily on her. Inside the apartment, she helped him to the sofa, then eased him down onto it. "Okay, now what?" she asked.

"I just need ice, some pillows and a couple of aspirin."

She found the bedroom and took the pillows off the bed, then found a bottle of aspirin in the bathroom's medicine cabinet and took a towel from the linen closet. As she collected her supplies, she took advantage of the opportunity to check out his apartment. The furniture wasn't particularly exciting—it looked like he had bought it by the room, and it was upholstered in a subtle earth-toned pattern—but what immediately caught her eye were the books. The walls of the living room and bedroom were lined with bookcases, filled with books. She didn't have time to read titles, but she noticed a variety ranging from popular paperbacks to big, hardcover scholarly books. Not only did the former jock know how to read, he was building his own personal library.

She returned to the living room to find him stretched out on the sofa, his eyes closed. "Are you sure aspirin will be enough?"

"It'll be fine."

She shook her head. "You know best." Then she gently lifted his knee and eased the pillows under it. "Is that better?" she asked.

He sighed. "Much. Thanks."

She put the aspirin bottle down on the coffee table, then went to the kitchen. The bin under the ice maker was full. "Do you have any plastic bags?" she called back to the living room.

"Look under the sink."

She found a plastic grocery bag and put some ice in it, then tied it shut. She wrapped the pack in the towel, then, as an afterthought, she filled a glass with water. Returning to the living room, she handed him the glass of water and placed the ice pack on his knee. He winced from the cold, then sighed and reached for the aspirin bottle and shook out two pills, which he swallowed with the help of some water. Maddy took the glass from him, then sat on the chair across from the sofa to observe him.

He looked a little pale, although he was looking better than he had back at the ballpark. Before she put the ice pack on his knee, she had noticed how badly it was swelling. "Are you sure you're okay? I can call a doctor."

"I told you, I'm fine," he snapped, then he shook his head slowly. "Sorry about that. I owe you an apology. I'm lucky you were there tonight. I don't know what I'd have done without your help." He raised himself on one elbow. "By the way, what were you doing there tonight?"

"The book said if participating in an athletic event didn't work, being a spectator was almost as good. Well, participating didn't work too well, and you had said there were some guys on your team, so I thought I'd give it a shot."

"And I ruined your chances by making you leave before you had a chance to meet anyone. Sorry about that, Maddy."

"That's okay. I don't think I would have had much success, anyway. After all, if you found one of your teammates obnoxiously jocklike, imagine how I'd feel."

"That is an interesting mental picture. What sport did you try, if you don't mind my asking?"

"Ice skating."

He sat up halfway. "Ice skating? What kind of men do you think you'd meet ice-skating? I didn't know you were into sequins on men."

He had to be feeling much better. This was sounding like the Derek she knew. "Hockey players ice-skate, too, you know. And I met a very nice man."

"I thought you said you struck out."

"I didn't say I struck out. I just didn't have great success. We spent the whole afternoon together, as a matter of fact."

"What happened?"

She sighed. "I need to work on my follow-through. He didn't seem to know he was supposed to ask me to get some coffee with him afterward, and I didn't think to ask him myself until he'd gone."

Derek nodded. "Snagged out at first."

"What's that supposed to mean?"

"It's a baseball expression. I'll have to explain it to you sometime."

"Don't bother. I doubt I'll be using it often in conversation, and I doubt I'll be getting too involved with someone who speaks in baseball-ese."

"Yeah, well, I am sorry your weekend turned out to be such a low point."

"Speak for yourself. You're the one lying there with a swollen knee. Your weekend won't be worth writing about."

He sighed and sank back against the sofa cushions. "We are quite a pair, aren't we? Stuck with nothing to do on a Saturday night." He stared up at the ceiling for a while, then rolled over onto his side and propped himself up on one elbow. "What do you say we do something?"

"Like what?" she asked, gesturing at his injured knee. "You need to stay off that leg."

"We could stay in, but still do something. We could order pizza and watch a movie. I've got a stack of tapes I've never watched."

She really didn't have any other ideas, and she didn't want to leave him alone in his condition, at least not until the worst of the pain went away. He was trying to act casual, but she could see the strain around his eyes. "Okay," she said at last. "But does this count as a date?"

He met her eyes and gave her a measuring look. "Not if you don't want it to," he said in a husky voice. She had to look away because she wasn't sure what her answer would be if he asked her what she wanted.

"I'll go order the pizza," she said. "Where's your phone?"

"In the kitchen. And there are some pizza coupons on the refrigerator door."

"What kind of pizza do you want?" she called back to him from the kitchen when she had found the phone.

"I'll eat anything."

She selected a pizza restaurant from the handful of coupons under the magnet on the refrigerator door and called to place her order. Then she returned to the living room.

"What did you order?" he asked.

"Pepperoni."

He raised an eyebrow. "You? Miss health queen? I'm shocked."

"And extra cheese, too. I feel like living dangerously. And after the exercise I got this afternoon, I'm entitled."

"Good for you. Now, if you'll do the honors of selecting a film for us. You'll find the tapes on the bookshelf over there." He pointed across the room to yet another bookshelf. Instead of books, its top shelf was filled with videotapes.

She was sure it wouldn't be too hard to find something fun to watch. He probably had a few action/adventure movies with lots of car chases, just what she wanted in a situation like this. But she was surprised not to find a single *Lethal Weapon* movie. Most of his collection consisted of foreign films with subtitles or British literary adaptations. Not that she didn't like that sort of thing herself, but these were the kinds of movies that started in-depth conversations, and she was beginning to think that might be a mistake, especially if she wasn't sure she wanted their relationship to progress much further. This was already too close to a date for comfort.

"Where did you get all these movies, and why?" she finally had to ask when curiosity overcame her.

"Not what you'd expect from a dumb jock, huh?"

She turned to face him. "Derek, I don't know what to expect from you anymore."

He gave her a half smile. "Good. Now, have you chosen anything?"

She shrugged and took a tape from the shelf. "What about *Howard's End?* I never saw that one."

"Neither did I. That's why I got the tape. I loved the book, but I never got around to seeing the movie."

"I suppose you'll want to analyze the implications of the movie and compare the movie to the book once it's over," she said as she walked back across the room and dropped the tape on the coffee table, then sat down cross-legged on the floor in front of the sofa.

"Maybe. Would that be a problem?"

She chewed on her lower lip. She had been superficial friends with him so long, it was almost scary getting to know him this well. But one look at him was enough to make her want to take the chance. How could she keep forgetting how gorgeous he was? And now she was discovering he was intelligent, too. "No problem. But I haven't read the book." She laughed, suddenly aware of how the roles had been reversed. She was beginning to feel like the dumb one. "Are you going to insist on shattering every stereotype I've ever held of you?"

"I don't know. What kinds of stereotypes have you held of me?"

"Do you really want to hear this?"

"Only if you want to say it."

She took a deep breath. Things were getting way too heavy, way too fast. He had a talent for that, she had noticed. That was just one of the stereotypes he kept shattering. No one could ever call him shallow.

"Okay, here's just one," she began. "I used to think you were just on the newspaper staff in college because you were some kind of sports star and your name would look good in the paper. I didn't even read your stories. Then I thought the same thing when you went to work for the *Journal*."

He nodded, his face impassive. "When did you first start reading my work?"

"When we started writing these columns. Then I started reading your sports stories, too."

"And?"

"And you're a good writer. There was some talent to go with that swagger, after all."

"I don't know why I never bothered all that time," she continued, more to herself than to him. "I think I just liked not having my opinions challenged, and I liked having a reason to argue with you."

"At least you acknowledged my existence on the staff. The others all probably thought the way you did, but they didn't even bother to speak to me."

The doorbell rang, shattering the mood and making Maddy jump. "That'll be the pizza," she said, getting up from the floor. "Enough introspection for one night."

He twisted around to get his wallet from his pocket. "Here's some money," he said, handing her a few bills. "This one's on me, in exchange for nursing services."

She started to argue, then remembered how little money she had taken with her that evening. She'd have to make him dinner sometime, she decided. She took the bills and went to the door to get the pizza. "I guess I should go get us some plates and something to drink," she said, placing the pizza box on the coffee table. "What do you have?"

"I think there's a bottle of something in the refrigerator."

"Okay, I'll be back in a second." As he had promised, there was a bottle of root beer in the refrigerator. She filled two glasses with ice, poured the root beer, then found a couple of plates and some paper towels and carried it all back to the living room, balancing the glasses on top of the plates. She let out her breath in a sigh of relief as she placed everything gently on the coffee table. "I hope you're impressed with my achievement there," she said with a wry smile. "I didn't spill a drop."

"Very impressive," he agreed, taking a sip from a glass of root beer. He put the glass back on the table, then pulled himself farther into a sitting position on the sofa. "Do you want to go ahead and start the movie?"

She turned on the television, inserted the tape into the VCR, then crawled back across the room on her hands and knees to the sofa. Taking a position with her back resting against the couch, she first handed Derek a slice of pizza on a plate, then took one herself. They ate and watched the movie in silence. Maddy surprised herself by becoming engrossed in the story. She would have thought there would be too many other distractions in this setting.

Then Derek leaned forward to get another slice of pizza, and his arm brushed her shoulder. She jumped as if she'd been electrocuted. "Let me get that for you," she whispered, wondering why her pulse had suddenly started racing. He had startled her, she decided as she put a slice of pizza on the plate and handed it to him. Then she took another slice for herself and tried once more to engross herself in the movie.

This time, it wasn't so easy. She had sat down too close to Derek's end of the sofa, so close she could feel the warmth radiating from his body and hear his soft breathing. Every fiber in her body tingled with awareness of his presence. She stole a sideways glance at him, but he just ate his pizza and stared at the television screen, seemingly oblivious to her presence. She returned her attention to the movie, wondering how she could be feeling such chemistry on her own.

Despite the movie's British Victorian sensibilities, it was rife with sexual tension, which didn't help Maddy much. When Derek finished his pizza and put his plate down on the coffee table he brushed her shoulder again, setting off another series of shock waves. As he moved into a more comfortable position, his thigh moved against the back of her neck. She would almost swear he was doing it on purpose.

Well, two could play at that game. She slouched down until her shoulders rested against the edge of the sofa cushions and the back of her head leaned against his leg. Then his hand moved against her hair in very deliberate, very gentle strokes. He was definitely doing that on purpose. She had to stifle her gasp of shock.

*Now what?* she thought. This situation had the potential to become rather interesting, but she wasn't sure what she wanted to happen next. She let him continue to stroke her hair while she fought to remain perfectly still. He removed his hand from her hair, but she hardly had a chance to relax before he was running the backs of his fingers across her shoulder and up her neck, then back down again. She couldn't completely stifle the low moan that emerged from the back of her throat. If he were deliberately trying to drive her stark raving mad, he couldn't have picked a better way.

All her nerves had gone from tingling to on fire, and goose bumps crept up her arms. If he didn't stop soon, she was going to dissolve into a mass of quivering flesh right there on his living room floor.

And he didn't stop. He kept stroking her neck and shoulder, sometimes teasing her earlobe with his thumb, sometimes pausing to give her shoulder a gentle squeeze. Her breathing grew shallow and ragged, just from the effect of his light touch. She never would have thought something so seemingly innocuous would have the potential to affect her so strongly.

Finally, she could take it no more. She turned toward him to tell him he had to stop, but she did so at a time when his hand was at the apex of its course up her neck. When she moved, she turned against his hand so that it cupped her chin. That hadn't been what she had in mind, but she very quickly forgot what she had in mind as she became locked in his gaze.

He stared at her as if he were drinking in every detail of her. There was a hungry look in his eyes she had never seen before. His hand on her chin gave a slight tug so that she moved forward, closer to him. She knew what would happen next. It wasn't entirely inevitable. She had the power to stop it. It would be so easy to stop it, easier now than later. But she remembered the kiss on her doorstep, and she didn't want to stop it. She parted her lips as they met his.

The kiss was not nearly as gentle as his touch had been. It was powerful and consuming, drawing her deeper and deeper into his spell. He moved his hand from her chin to the back of her neck and held her more closely against him. His other arm gathered her up onto the sofa next to him so that their bodies pressed together from head to toe.

"Derek," she panted when he released her enough for her to breathe again. "What about the movie?"

"I've read the book," he answered in a throaty whisper before claiming her mouth again. His lips were warm and moist against hers, and when his tongue touched hers, it threatened to start a blaze within her. She couldn't believe this was happening to her, but she didn't want it to end. She clutched his shirt in her left hand, clinging to him although he had shown no sign of letting her go. When he did release her mouth, it was to trail blazing kisses down her neck to her collarbone. She arched her back, allowing him more access to skin that yearned for his touch, but pulled her head back down again to kiss her lips once more.

He pulled her body even closer to his, then shifted himself so that he was lying halfway on top of her, pressing her into the sofa cushions. She sighed at the comforting, warm weight of his body resting on hers, and he answered with a groan.

But it wasn't a groan of pleasure, it was a groan of pain. He ended the kiss abruptly and released her to clutch with both hands at his injured knee. "Damn," he grunted. She helped ease him into a more comfortable position and replaced the ice pack that had fallen off.

"Are you okay?" she asked, clutching at his hand.

"I'll be fine." He gave her hand a squeeze, then sighed. "Sorry about that. I guess it wasn't such a good idea."

Not meeting his eyes, she said, "Good idea, just bad timing. Maybe you'd better take it easy for a while."

"That would probably be a very good idea."

Maddy resumed her earlier seat on the floor next to the sofa, but she didn't relinquish her hold on his hand. After what had just happened, it was pointless to try to watch the movie, but she stared at the television, anyway, grateful for the excuse to sit still and let her mind wander. She wouldn't believe it had really happened if her heart wasn't still pounding and if her lips didn't feel so swollen from Derek's kisses. And they had been such kisses. . . .

"Maddy," Derek whispered after a few moments. "I just want you to know I didn't plan that. In fact, there wasn't much thinking or planning involved. I don't know what happened."

Before he could say anything more, she turned around and placed a finger against his lips. "Stop that," she scolded. "You don't have to apologize. It happened, and I rather enjoyed it. There's only one problem," she added with a smile.

"What's that?"

"I think we sort of have to count this as a date. After all, we did meet at the ballpark, we had dinner and a movie, and we kissed. That makes two for us. If we keep this up, we'll tie."

"And we'll never hear the end of it in the newsroom."

"So, how are we going to write about this?" she asked.

"Do we have to include this as part of the assignment, or is it just us? I thought we could just write about the other people we struck out with."

"You're right. I think this is just us. What's happening here, Derek?"

He ran a hand through his hair. "I think it's been happening a long time. We just weren't aware of it."

She nodded. "Maybe that's it." They sat in silence a few more minutes, ignoring the movie that continued to play on the television. "Derek," Maddy said after a while, "I just thought of something."

"What?" he asked, reaching under her hair to rub the back of her neck.

She steeled herself against the sensation. Now would not be a good time to start that again. "I just realized I don't have a way to get home. I don't think I could get home from here on my bike."

"Oh, yeah. And I don't think it would be a good idea for you to spend the night here."

"Probably not," she agreed. If she had to be near him much longer, she wasn't sure what might happen, and she wasn't prepared for that yet.

"Why don't you just take my truck home, then come back in the morning. I should be able to drive you home by then."

"Boy, you must really trust me if you're willing to let me take that truck off by myself."

"Yeah, I trust you. I'm not excited about the idea of the truck being parked overnight in your neighborhood, but I trust your driving."

"Well, I think I'll be heading home," she said, rising to her feet. "Are you sure you're okay? Do you need help with anything else before I go?"

"I'll be okay," he assured her. "This happens more often than you think. I'll be limping tomorrow, but I'll be back to normal by Monday."

She nodded. "Well, call me if you need me."

"The keys are there on the coffee table. Just take the truck keys off the ring."

She picked up the key ring and slipped the truck keys off, then dropped the rest of the keys back on the table. "Thanks for dinner and the movie and, well, everything else." She bent over him and kissed his forehead. "I'll see you in the morning."

She turned to leave, but he called after her. "Maddy?" She turned back to face him. "Thank you for being there when I needed help."

She nodded. "I'm glad I was there." Before he could say anything else, she slipped out through the door and shut it behind her.

The night was cool, but she rolled down the truck windows as she drove down the highway toward downtown. The brisk wind streaming through the windows to caress her face soothed her churning emotions and doused the flames Derek's kisses had started burning within her. She hadn't planned on this when she asked Derek to join her on this assignment. She'd had no idea he would be the one she found when she went on a search for romance. She wondered what he thought about what was happening between them. They needed to talk, but she wasn't sure she was ready to face the issue, not yet. They still had one more chapter in the book to get through.

She pulled into a parking space in front of her apartment building, making sure to roll up the windows and lock the doors. Derek would never forgive her if his truck were stolen while in her possession. Once she entered her apartment, she knew sleep would be pointless. She was too much on edge. She switched on her radio, keeping the volume low out of consideration for her neighbors, even though the raucous rock music sounded strange playing so softly.

Normally when she felt this restless, she danced until she grew tired, but she didn't feel like dancing tonight. She curled up on her futon and picked up a book, but the words just swam before her eyes. She put the book down and picked up a spiral notebook and a pen and began to write.

*Hers:*

Just as it's kind of pointless to try to find someone compatible at a nightclub that plays music you don't like, it's rather pointless to try to meet someone through an athletic event if you're completely unathletic.

I am not an athletic person. I like to say that I don't do anything that involves a spherical object being hurled in my general direction. I don't even watch sports on television, except when they have figure skating on during the Winter Olympics.

I decided that since ice skating is part of the Olympics, it counts as a sport. So, I headed to the mall one Saturday afternoon to see who I could find. The ice rink was crowded, with a few proficient skaters, a few more like myself who were doing well to remain upright and a lot of obnoxious little kids born with skates on their feet who darted in and around the rest of us. One of those kids inadvertently brought me together with Mr. Wonderful.

Mr. Wonderful was just what I was looking for: tall, handsome and a good skater. He gave me a few pointers and kept me upright as we skated around the rink. We spent the rest of the day together. Then, as we left . . . *nothing happened!*

A friend of mine who is fluent in baseball metaphors said I was snagged out at first base, whatever that means. What I do know is Mr. Wonderful obviously hadn't seen the script that called for him to invite me for coffee and cheesecake after skating, and I wasn't good enough at improvising to invite him myself.

The moral of this story is that anyone can find someone compatible anywhere. Clinging to stereotypes can make you blind to someone who could be perfect for you. The trick is to be open to the possibilities, then be prepared to follow through when you have the chance. Don't let Mr. Wonderful disappear into the hordes of shoppers with his skates slung over his back. Or maybe it wasn't meant to be.

*His:*

I'm a very athletic person, so I thought this one would be easy for me, definitely easier than finding someone compatible at a symphony concert. I was right. The first night I played with a neighborhood softball team, I hit it off rather well with the first basewoman. After our victory, it was only natural that we go out to celebrate.

It was then that I realized I was wrong. Just because a woman can recognize the wishbone formation in football or snag a line drive on the fly, it doesn't mean I have much in common with her, even though I can do those things. There is more to my personality than that. Sports can sustain a conversation for one evening, but there has to be something more to sustain a relationship.

I guess I'm still looking for a woman who can snag a line drive on the fly and discuss Shakespeare, but until I find one, I'd rather have the woman who can discuss Shakespeare.

P.S. For those who've been calling me a loser who can't get a date, I was the one who dumped this woman. I just thought you ought to know.

# 12

Maddy finished reading Derek's column and smiled as she laid the newspaper on her desk. "What about E. M. Forster?" she said softly, shoving the paperback copy of *Howard's End* out of her way as she rummaged through her knapsack for The Book, as she had come to think of it.

The trade-size paperback was now dog-eared and worn. "We've been through a lot together, haven't we?" she said to the book, then quickly glanced around the newsroom to make sure no one had seen her talking to a book. Unfortunately, Rhona was standing right behind her. "Rhona, this assignment has been hazardous to my mental health, and now you have proof," she said.

"You're almost done, aren't you?"

"Yeah, and it's a good thing, too. I'm afraid I'm losing interest."

"Don't tell me you're losing interest in romance," her editor said, perching on the corner of Maddy's desk.

"Not in romance per se, but in the assignment. I'm not too excited about the idea of finding a man right now."

"Could that be because you've found someone?"

"Maybe," Maddy hedged.

"You've been holding out on me, Maddy. When did this happen? Which chapter was it?"

Maddy started to say that she had found him with the book's title, but she bit her tongue. The last thing she and Derek needed as they explored their tenuous beginning of a relationship was interference from Rhona. "Oh, sometime along the way," she said.

"So you think this is the right one?"

"I don't know. I just know that no one else has come close, so far."

Rhona patted her shoulder and slipped off her perch on the desk. "You've just got one more chapter. Who knows what can happen. They've probably saved the best tip for last."

Chewing on her lower lip, Maddy picked up the book and flipped through to the last chapter, then began to read.

*If you ask all the happy couples you know how they met, chances are most will tell you they met through friends. Statistically, that's how most couples meet. To meet the right person, you just need to enlist the help of your friends.*

*Let your friends, both married and single, know you're looking. They'll immediately start thinking about who they know who'll be good for you. You may have to kiss a few toads this way, but you're sure to eventually find your handsome prince or beautiful princess.*

*One way to speed up the process is to take matters into your own hands. Get together with a few single friends and throw a party. Have all the single people you know invite all the single people they know. You're sure to find someone right in that crowd.*

Maddy tossed the book onto her desk with a disgusted grunt. She knew what setups were like. She always got set up with the men her friends felt sorry for. It kind of made her wonder if they felt the same way about her. Then there was the friend she had known in college who had claimed to love playing matchmaker, then had proceeded to sink her claws into every man Maddy pointed out that she would like to meet. "I might as well write this column now," she said to herself. "I can already tell how this is likely to turn out."

Her desk phone rang, and she answered it with a perky, "This is Maddy."

"Well, if it isn't the Mad Hatter herself," came the voice on the other end of the line.

Maddy felt her cheeks grow warm and her pulse start racing at the sound of his voice. Sunday morning had been terribly awkward when she went to return his truck. They had avoided looking at each other and had barely spoken as he drove her back home. Now it sounded like he, at least, had gotten over the worst of the awkwardness. She hoped it wasn't because he was putting what happened behind him.

"What kind of torture does The Book have planned for us this time?" he asked.

"You're probably going to hate this one as much as I do. It says most couples meet through friends and that you should ask all your friends to get you together with anyone they know who might be suitable."

"That could take forever, just working my way through the list of women my mother thinks I should meet."

"You, too, huh? There is a shortcut. It says to throw a party, invite all your single friends and have them invite their single friends."

"It sounds miserable, but at least we'd be getting it over with quickly. I guess I'll host, since my place is a bit bigger. I'll even invite a few of the guys on the football team."

"That should be a big draw for my friends. When do you want to do this?"

"What about Friday night at eight?"

"That should work. Need any help from me?"

"Just bring some drinks and snacks, and I'm sure you have a few good tapes."

"Yeah, I can take care of the music. I'll get there about six to help you get set up."

"I won't lie and say I'm looking forward to it, but I am looking forward to seeing you."

"Me, too," she whispered into the phone, hoping no one else noticed the way she was grinning giddily. He hadn't changed his mind about her, after all. "I guess I'd better start making a few phone calls, and so should you. Try to invite a few literate guys who like to dance."

"They're in short supply, but I'll see what I can do. Any requests for yourself?"

"I think you have that taken care of." Maddy's voice shook as she said it. That was an awfully bold statement for her to make. She held her breath for his reply.

"Okay, just as long as you show up," he said. "See you."

Maddy hung up the phone and began flipping through her address book. She almost wished she had been honest with Rhona so she could have ended this farce, but who knew, she might meet someone better in the crowd. Then she remembered Derek and decided that was unlikely. She wasn't even likely to notice anyone else that night.

But at the same time, she was nervous about being around Derek again. Things were happening too quickly for her, and she still wasn't sure if she really wanted a relationship with him. She knew she liked his kisses, that she liked being touched by him. She just wasn't sure she was ready to open herself up to all the emotions he seemed to inspire in her. At least there would be other people around Friday night, so she wouldn't have to worry too much about being alone with him.

* * *

Derek rearranged the plastic cups and bags of potato chips on his kitchen counter one more time. He couldn't remember the last time he'd thrown a party. It had probably been back when he was in college. He wasn't sure now why he had gone along with this crazy plot. As far as he was concerned, he had found the woman he wanted to get to know better. He wasn't interested in looking for anyone new, and he certainly wasn't interested in Maddy finding anyone. They should have just come clean with what had happened between them and skipped the final chapter. But he supposed they had to check out the book's final chapter as a service to their readers.

"Just this one night, and then it's all over," he reminded himself. In retrospect, he couldn't complain about what had happened in the course of the assignment. It had been the best thing to happen to him. That didn't mean he had to like the things the assignment had required him to do. This party promised to be the worst of all. It had taken some work on his part to convince his friends to come. He hoped Maddy had come through on her invitations.

A knock at his door interrupted his thoughts. He left the counter arrangement the way it was and went to the door. "Here, give me a hand with this," Maddy said as soon as he opened the door. She shoved an armful of paper grocery sacks at him and he staggered under the unexpected weight. "Whew," she said, taking off her black fedora and wiping her arm across her forehead before replacing the hat. "I thought I was going to drop those before I got to your door. I'll take one back now," she added, relieving him of one of the bags.

"What do you have in here, rocks?" he asked as he followed her to the kitchen.

"No, drinks. I got a couple of two-quart bottles of just about every soft drink, plus a few bottles of wine and a couple of six packs of beer. I hope that will be enough."

"We'll be swimming, because I got the same thing."

She dropped her burden on the countertop and stretched her shoulders. He put down his bag and started unloading the contents of both bags into the refrigerator. He could feel her eyes on him as he rearranged the refrigerator to take the additional drinks. "How's the knee?" she asked. "I didn't notice much of a limp."

"It's back to normal, more or less, but I'm afraid my softball days are over. Maybe I'll take up golf." He was grateful for the small talk that gave him the chance to get his brain in gear. He didn't know why, but it had quit working the moment she stepped in the door. He knew she had been having a growing effect on him, but this was getting out of hand. Right now, if he had any say in the matter, he'd call the whole party off so he could have her to himself.

"Who says you have to have a sport?" she asked. "There are plenty of other things to do with your time, believe me."

"I was joking," he assured her. "I have more than enough to keep myself busy."

"Like what?" she challenged. "I've asked you before, but you always sidestep the question. It's not illegal, is it?"

"What else did you bring?" he asked with a malicious grin. "I hope you brought some good music. My collection is somewhat limited."

She glared at him for a second, then grinned, reached into one of the sacks and brought out a cassette carrying case. "Will twenty tapes be enough?"

"I hope so. With any luck, everyone will pair off and head out quickly."

"You're not looking forward to this, are you," she asked, a smile tugging at the corners of her mouth.

He leaned back against the counter. "Not really. I haven't been comfortable with the whole assignment. I don't like the feeling of putting myself out on some kind of market."

"I suppose charity bachelor auctions are completely out of the question for you, then."

He shuddered. "My worst nightmare."

She patted him on the arm. "Don't worry. If you get forced into one, I'd bid on you. I probably wouldn't win because I don't have much money, but I would at least try to drive the price up. Now, let's get some of these snacks out in bowls."

Derek watched her for a moment, dumbfounded. She was being just as breezy and bouncy as usual, while he felt almost suffocated by the tension in the air. After what had happened—or almost happened—between them the last time they were together, he would have expected something different from her, but she didn't seem to be feeling a thing.

"I hope you got some cute guys to come," she continued as she poured potato chips into a large bowl. "Otherwise, I'm in trouble with my friends because I promised them something special. Not that I'd mind myself," she added with a wink.

If he had his way, he'd lock her in his bedroom until everyone else left, he thought, surprising himself with the vehemence of his feelings. He never would have imagined himself being so possessive or jealous. But all he had to do was look at her to feel an intense longing to take off that silly hat so he could see her eyes, then kiss her until both of them lost their senses. He blinked as if to wipe the mental picture from his consciousness and turned away from her to open another bag of chips. This was going to be a long night.

It was a very long night, but at least it seemed to be going well, he thought later that evening as he opened a bag of pretzels to replenish a bowl. From the living room he heard sounds of conversation and laughter. A few of his friends appeared to have hooked up with some of Maddy's friends, and so far, at least one couple had gone off on their own to see a movie that had just opened.

As for himself, Derek wasn't particularly intrigued by any of the women at the party. At any other time, he might have been, but he couldn't stop thinking of Maddy. She didn't spend much time with any of the other men at the party, but he wasn't sure if that was because she didn't find them interesting or if it was because she was too busy with her duties as hostess.

He picked up the refilled bowl and headed back to the living room. Maddy passed him on the way, carrying an empty bowl. "I wish you had enough room for a dance floor," she hissed. "I haven't had a chance to sit down and talk all night. They're all just talking and eating."

"At least they're talking and we don't have to worry about deadly silences," he reminded her.

She rolled her eyes at him and continued into the kitchen. He placed the bowl of pretzels on the coffee table and looked up to see another pair leaving. There were only eight people left, not counting Maddy and himself. One couple sat huddled together on one end of the sofa. Another were practically on top of each other in the middle. At the other end of the sofa, a woman sat, with one of Derek's friends sitting on the floor at her feet. The fourth couple stood by the bookcase on the far side of the room, their heads close together. Derek rolled his eyes and picked up another bowl that needed replenishing. He could see what Maddy meant about needing something else for them to do. They all ate mechanically as they talked.

With a sigh, he returned to the kitchen. Maddy looked up from refilling an ice bucket and groaned. "Are you starting to feel like you've been invaded by vultures?" she asked.

"Oh, I don't know. I don't think I'd worry too much if I were having any success here."

She grinned. "I'm glad you feel that way. I was beginning to think it was just me. I had this feeling I had to be the most unattractive woman here."

"That's definitely not the case," he assured her, delighting in the pleased flush that spread across her cheeks. "Besides, even if we're total failures in the attraction department, it looks like we're complete successes at matchmaking. Everyone has paired off nicely."

"I don't know that we're failures in attracting others," she said. "Maybe it's just that your friends aren't interested in me, and vice versa."

"But they're definitely interested in each other."

A call from the living room verified that. "'Bye, Derek" came a voice. "Thanks for the party. This was great."

"Yeah, thanks Maddy," a female voice echoed. "I owe you one. This was a great idea." Then came the sound of the front door shutting.

"With any luck, the rest of them will leave soon," Maddy whispered, a conspiratorial gleam in her eyes.

"What do you think it would take to chase them away?" Derek whispered back, edging closer so they could hear each other without their words traveling back to the living room.

"What if we quit refilling the bowls?"

"Good idea. It's our party. Let's go in there and enjoy it." He held out his hand to her, and she took it. Her touch set off a chain reaction in him, so much so that he almost decided to stay in the kitchen alone with her, but she was already moving forward. He followed her reluctantly.

She sat in the chair next to the sofa, and he sat on the floor next to her, but none of the others in the room appeared to notice their arrival. Derek and Maddy exchanged smiles and shrugs. Sitting there surrounded by people who were oblivious to them was uncomfortable, but Derek was tired. He leaned against the side of Maddy's chair. She reached down and gave his shoulder a squeeze, making him wish even more that his guests would leave.

The couple standing by the bookcase seemed to come to an agreement, returned to the rest of the group and quickly made their goodbyes. The others followed their lead. Derek and Maddy rose to see them all off. At last, Derek shut the door with a triumphant grin. Maddy sagged wearily against him, and he slipped an arm around her waist. "What time is it?" she asked.

He looked at his watch. "Believe it or not, it's only eleven."

"I thought it had to be midnight at the earliest. I can't remember the last time I went to a party that ended by eleven." She moved over to the couch and sank down in one corner, then took a throw pillow and clutched it to her chest.

There was definitely something going on here, Derek decided, taking a seat on the other end of the sofa. She had been jumpy all evening, but she was really closing herself off now that they were alone.

"Maddy, is something wrong?" he asked.

"Wrong? No. Why would anything be wrong?" Her voice shook, giving lie to her protestations.

"Oh, I don't know. I just thought…" He let his voice trail off, unsure exactly what he thought.

"I guess it's just the sting of rejection," she mused out loud, as if still considering his question. "It's kind of sad to be someplace like this and not attract anyone."

She hadn't gone completely without attracting someone, he thought, but she didn't seem to want to hear that at this time. "Don't think of us as social failures, think of us as very successful matchmakers," he reminded her. "When was the last time you saw people pairing up so neatly? Usually there's at least one man and one woman left out, and they want nothing to do with each other. We could go into business."

"Don't mention that to Rhona, or she'll have us start another series where we play matchmakers to the city," she groaned, leaning farther back into the sofa cushions. Derek noticed that she was relaxing slightly. Maybe it was just the stress of the party getting to her. "I've had enough of these special assignments. I'm looking forward to getting back to normal."

"Me, too. It will be good to have more spare time again. I've been falling behind."

She turned toward him. "Falling behind in what?" she asked. "And this time you're going to answer the question."

He stared at her for a moment, trying to measure what he knew of her. He had told no one at the newspaper about his ambitions as an author, but if he was going to trust anyone he knew it would be her. "I do some writing," he said, with as nonchalant a shrug as he could manage.

"I know that, you're a reporter. But you don't spend all your spare time doing that."

"No, I do some other writing. Fiction."

Her eyebrows shot up. "Really? What kind of fiction?"

"I've published a few short stories, nothing major. And I'm working on a novel."

"Derek, that's fascinating. And all this time I've been calling you a dumb jock. Why didn't you tell me before? That would have shut me up."

"Would it? Or would you have teased me?" She didn't answer, only chewed her lower lip. He squeezed her shoulders, pulling her closer to him. "I think we both just had to get to know each other better. In fact, I don't think we can consider ourselves failures in this project. We found each other, didn't we?"

She looked up at him for a long moment, during which his pulse throbbed in his temples. He had no idea how she really felt, and he could almost hear her telling him he was crazy. But she didn't. "Yes, I guess we did," she whispered back to him. Then she grinned. "Okay, Newman, what else do I not know about you? Is there anything else you've been hiding?"

"Just don't open any closets around here. Now it's your turn. What is there about you I don't know?"

She gave him a look of feigned innocence, her eyes wide, as she said, "Who, me? I'm an open book."

"Seriously, Maddy."

She frowned in thought, running the fingers of her right hand through the fringe on the pillow, then said, "Okay, I have to admit it. I like reviewing nightclubs, writing about new bands and, yes, even writing fluff about finding the perfect mate. It's fun. I just used to say all that stuff about serious reporting because it was what I thought I was supposed to say. I don't think I'd change what I'm doing if I had the chance." She shrugged. "So maybe that makes me a bit of an airhead. So sue me. And, believe it or not, I'm not a total party girl. I really only go out when I'm reviewing something. Otherwise, I'm as bad a homebody as you are."

"And what do you do at home?"

"Nothing nearly as interesting or worthwhile as what you do. I'm addicted to mystery novels. I curl up with one, stay up half the night to finish it, then sleep with at least one light on because I get edgy. I guess I have an overactive imagination."

He shook his head. "And to think, I never knew."

She laughed. "It's not like it's a major revelation. And does knowing those things really change anything about us? We're still the same people."

"But we had to bother to look at each other."

"There is that," she agreed. Then they both sat in silence for a long moment. Derek could feel the tension between them, so tangible he would have sworn he could reach up and feel it as a solid barrier. At the same time, he felt closer to Maddy than he ever had before. Something had happened between them—was happening between them—and although he didn't want to force it, he didn't want to let it go.

He eased closer to her until they were almost touching. She didn't edge away, but her eyes were wide. She must be feeling this as much as he was, he thought. Perhaps that explained her sudden fear. "I'm glad we got the chance to do this assignment," he said, keeping his tone as neutral as possible. "It's been good getting to know you better."

She smiled and nodded. "Yeah, it's been great. I'm glad we're friends now." He cringed at the word *friends,* wondering if that meant that was all she wanted. But she hadn't kissed him like she only wanted to be friends. He slipped an arm around her shoulders and gave her a squeeze. She didn't protest or try to move away, so he kept his arm around her shoulders and leaned back against the sofa cushions.

They didn't speak for a while. He was too busy concentrating on the warmth of her snuggled up against him in the shelter of his arm to even think of anything else to say. She felt right there, as if she belonged. He glanced down at her to find her looking up at him. They held eye contact for another long moment. He felt he was drowning in the gray-green depths of her eyes. At last, he could wait no longer.

"God, Maddy, why did it take us so long?" he whispered hoarsely as he lowered his mouth to hers. The kiss was the sweetest thing he had ever tasted, probably because he had been anticipating it for a week—for years, if he were honest with himself. He pulled away, well aware of where this would lead if he got started, and she backed off, as well. As close as he was to her, he could feel her trembling.

"Oh, Derek, I just don't know about this," she whispered. "I think this is happening too fast for me."

# 13

#### ━━◆━━

Maddy chanced a glance at Derek's face, then wished she hadn't. He looked shocked. It probably wasn't fair for her to lead him on like that, only to shove him away now. If only he knew that she felt the passion between them as strongly as he did. What he hadn't known was that right now, she was scared to death. She had barely become accustomed to thinking of her longtime adversary as a real friend. Thinking of him as a lover was too much for her to consider, although she had thought of little else the past week.

"This is happening so fast," she repeated as he sat up, helping her up with a tug on her hand.

"Fast?" he said, dumbfounded. "We've known each other for more than five years."

"Have we? Or did we really just meet? A little more than a month ago you were just a dumb ex-jock sportswriter who was too good-looking to be true to me, and to you I was just a flighty party girl with supposed aspirations of being a serious journalist. We both feel a bit rejected after what we've gone through, so naturally we turn to each other. I don't want to go any further if this isn't for real."

He shook his head. "Maddy, I really don't know what to say. I can't guarantee you that anything is for real. We have no way of knowing how this will work out. What I can guarantee you is that I find you very attractive and very interesting, and I want to know every detail about you. I want to spend as much time as possible with you, and I feel lost without you. One thing that book doesn't say is that we're all having to take chances all the time. There's no formula for finding the right person."

"If only it were that easy," she said with a sigh. "I guess what I'm afraid of is messing up a perfectly good friendship." She took one of his hands in both of hers. She had never noticed just how big his hands were. It took both of her hands to completely surround one of his hands. She ran her thumb lightly over his knuckles, then turned his hand over and traced the lines on his palm.

"You're a good friend, Derek, and I value that," she whispered. "I can't think of anyone else I could have gone through this crazy assignment with." She looked up at him and allowed herself a smile. "You know, I first chose you to work with me on this to get back at you. Now I'm glad I did."

"There's no reason we have to stop being friends," he said. "That's one of the things I like most about you. You're my friend. It's that friendship that was missing from every other relationship we've tried to strike up in this assignment."

"But what if things don't work out? Can we keep being friends after that?"

He pulled his hand from her grasp and gripped her shoulders, forcing her to look at him directly. "Are you predicting failure?" he asked. "What kind of friendship can we hope to have if we can't even expect a relationship to work out right? We've known each other for so long."

She had to admit he was right, and it would be so easy to agree with him. "But why did it take us so long, then, if it's right? In school, we couldn't get along at all."

"I think it took so long because we were never really looking at each other. I hate to admit it, but that stupid book was right. We managed to find someone through it, but probably not in the way the author intended."

"I wonder if the supermarket thing ever really worked for anyone," she asked, in a halfhearted attempt at a joke.

"I'm sure it must have. But I don't know that it works when you're looking for it. It's like we kept saying in our columns, when you're so conscious of an agenda, nothing you do is fun anymore, and you become more critical of people you might like once you get to know them, if you gave them a chance."

"You're probably right about that," she agreed softly. If she wasn't careful, he would have her lowering her guard completely by the time he was through. The prospect both scared and excited her.

"What would you have thought if you'd seen me walking that dachshund?" he asked with a wry grin.

She chuckled in spite of herself at the mental image. "Cute dog, cute guy, but they obviously don't match."

"Cute guy, huh?" he asked with a roguish grin as he bent to kiss her again. She stiffened, but she didn't back away. Excitement was beginning to win over fear. She wanted his kiss, even as she feared it.

The first kiss was playful. The second was serious. Then he removed her hat so he could kiss her more thoroughly. By this time, he was beyond gentle, wooing kisses. He kissed her as though he were claiming her for his own. She opened her lips against his, yielding to his exploration of her mouth. As he kissed her, he ran one hand across her silky hair, then down her back. She arched her back at his touch, pressing her breasts even closer to his chest. The last remnants of her fear dissipated, leaving desire in their wake. This felt so very right.

Slowly, he bent her back onto the sofa, bearing her beneath him as he eased her down against the cushions. He brushed her hair off her forehead, whispering, "You're so beautiful, Madeline. Why do you hide under those crazy hats?"

She chuckled, despite the intimate setting. "It's just a habit, a way to establish my identity and make up for bad hair days. But if you don't like my hats, I suppose I could do without them."

"I like your hats, just take them off around me so I can see you."

She bit her lip and frowned up at him. "Does that mean we're going to be around each other?"

"After this?" he asked, indicating with a sweep of his hand their intimate position, bodies pressed against each other, faces almost touching. "I would hope so. Unless you object?"

"Not in the least," she breathed.

He released her shoulders to circle her waist with one arm as he cradled the back of her head with his other hand. She ran her hand across his shoulder, feeling the strength of his finely hewn muscles, then up his neck to weave her fingers through his tousled blond hair. "Oh, Derek," she whispered when his lips left her mouth to nuzzle her earlobe.

"Don't say anything else, Maddy," he warned between kisses.

"I wasn't going to complain. I wanted to say that I like this." She gasped as he hit a sensitive spot. "I *really* like this."

"Well, in that case..." he murmured as he eased her back against the sofa cushions. She linked her fingers behind his neck to draw him to her. They kissed, tasting each others' lips and lingering with each contact.

With a deep groan, he settled himself more firmly over her. His weight on top of her gave her a strange feeling of security, as if nothing could reach her in his presence. She wrapped one leg around him to hold him tighter to her. She could feel his heart beating against hers where his chest pressed against her breasts.

He teased her lips with his tongue. She flicked his tongue with hers, inviting him to come farther within her. He accepted the invitation with a bold thrust of his tongue into her mouth. A thrill shot through her, and she twined her fingers in his hair. She felt a great sense of loss when he withdrew, but she soon forgot her disappointment when he ran his lips down her neck to her collarbone. He reached between them to open first one button of her blouse, then the next and the next, his lips following closely behind his fingers. She gasped when he slipped his hand into her blouse to caress her breast. He ran his thumb across her nipple, sending shivers up and down her spine.

"Oh, Maddy," he breathed, returning his lips to hers to kiss her with a passion she never might have expected from him before tonight. She allowed herself to melt against him. This was so right.

When he laid another trail of kisses down her neck to her breast, she thought she might spontaneously combust, but when he cupped his hand around her breast, edged aside her bra and lowered his mouth to her budding nipple, she knew she would explode. She arched her back and gripped him even more tightly with her legs.

He ran his tongue back, forth and around her nipple, then sucked ever so slightly. She dug her fingers into his shoulders, steeling herself against the impulse to cry out. He raised his head to look her in the face. His eyes were bright, as if feverish, and a sheen of sweat covered his face.

"Maddy?" he asked hoarsely, leaving the question dangling in the air.

"Yes, please," she panted.

"Then I suggest we adjourn to someplace more comfortable." Before she was aware of what was happening, he had rolled off her and scooped her up in his arms. It was just as well, she thought as he carried her to the bedroom. She wasn't sure her legs would support her weight.

He laid her gently on the bed, then eased himself down next to her. "Where were we?" he whispered.

"Somewhere around here," she breathed, reaching to unfasten his shirt buttons. She undid one button before he caught her wrist.

"Are you sure of this?" he asked. "If you're worried about still being able to be friends, this is the point of no return."

She swallowed hard. She was beginning to shiver, but more from desire than from nerves. "I have no doubts," she said at last. "I want so much more than a friendship."

He nodded and released her wrist. With trembling hands, she continued to unbutton his shirt. His chest was as well-muscled as she would have expected from his general build, and it was covered with a sprinkling of finely curling hair that glowed silvery blond in the light streaming through the blinds from the street lamp outside.

Without saying a word, he shrugged off his shirt, then reached to undo the last few buttons of her blouse. She let it slide off her shoulders, then reached behind her back to unfasten her bra. She slipped the straps off her shoulders, then could bear the separation from Derek no longer and threw her arms around his neck. He enfolded her in his arms, and the feel of his skin against hers was enough to ignite further the fire that burned within her. They kissed feverishly, allowing their hands to explore each other's bare skin.

When the desire had built so high neither of them could contain it any longer, they parted for a brief moment to shed the rest of their clothing, then returned to each other's arms. Derek ran one hand lightly up one of Maddy's legs, from the bend of her knee up past her waist, leaving gooseflesh in his wake. "Mmm, so soft," he breathed into her ear. She let her own hands roam across his muscular back and luxuriated in the hard, strong feel of him.

Resting most of his weight on his elbows, he moved on top of her. She knew he was sparing her the bulk of his weight, but she couldn't bear even that much distance between them. She wrapped her arms around him and drew him down to her so that they were flesh-to-flesh, blending the lines of where her body ended and his began. To keep him against her, she locked her legs around his.

He brushed the sweat-dampened hair from her forehead and kissed her, exploring her mouth fully with his tongue. She then let her own tongue reach into him, becoming bolder at the groan of pleasure that elicited from him.

The feel of him against her made a deep, longing ache grow in her. She had to fill that ache, or she was sure she would die. "Now, please," she gasped.

He didn't need to ask what she meant. He simply nodded, kissed her again, then moved against her. She cried out as a thrill shot through her the instant their bodies joined, then let herself go to the building rhythm beating between them. It grew harder, faster, more feverish until she could take no more, then it built again. At last, it exploded, and they lay spent in each other's arms.

She stroked his sweat-slicked skin, then unsuccessfully fought back an inappropriate giggle.

"What is it?" he asked. "I didn't think it was all that funny."

"I was just remembering something."

He nibbled at her earlobe. "And what might that be?"

"Is this what you had in mind for the third date?"

Then he laughed softly, and as close as they were, his chuckle echoed through her body. "Not at the time, but I do see the appeal."

"So how does this affect the bet?" she asked. "I believe this is three dates in every sense of the concept. Who wins?"

"Why worry about that now?" he asked, his voice rough with desire as he proceeded to give her plenty of other things to think about.

Maddy sighed and stretched, luxuriating in the comfort of a firm mattress beneath her. Consciousness returned to her slowly, but even in her drowsy state, she knew something was different. She shouldn't be this comfortable. Her futon was lumpy and uneven. This could only mean that she wasn't asleep in her own bed. She opened her eyes to see an unfamiliar room. Then she saw her own bare shoulder peeking out from underneath the sheets, and memory flooded back to her in a rush.

But where was Derek? She could see from the dent in the pillow next to her that he had been there, but how could he just get up and leave her alone in his bed after last night? It had meant something to her. She would have hoped that it meant at least something to him. She became aware of the faint smell of bacon and coffee, and her anger faded. She smiled when she noticed the terry-cloth robe laid across the foot of the bed. Suddenly hungry, she wrapped the robe around herself and padded barefoot into the kitchen.

Derek stood in front of the stove, expertly flipping pancakes on a skillet. He wore faded jeans and a white T-shirt, and his blond hair was tousled into a mop of curls. He hummed softly to himself as he tended the stove. Maddy had to bite her lip as unexpected tears welled in her eyes. She had never had a man make breakfast for her. "Good morning," she said when she could trust her voice. "You've been holding out on me again, Newman. I didn't know you could cook."

He looked up, and his face broke into a grin when he saw her standing there. "With my appetite, my mother made me learn. I'm no gourmet, but I can make a decent breakfast."

"Mmm, it smells wonderful," she said, crossing the room to stand behind him. She wrapped her arms around his waist and pressed her cheek against his back. "You didn't have to make me breakfast, you know," she murmured.

"Yes, I did," he said, turning the bacon over. He let the bacon sizzle for a few seconds before continuing. "The way I see it, not only did we both win the bet, we both lost, too. As I recall, we owe each other some servitude. I just wanted a head start on my end of the deal."

"We could call it even, you know."

He turned around within her grasp and planted a kiss on her forehead. "But this is so much more fun." He turned back around and flipped a pancake. "How many do you think you'll eat?"

Her rumbling stomach answered for her. "I'm starving," she confessed. "I didn't get a chance to eat last night and ..."

"And we burned up a lot of energy," he finished for her. She was glad to see that he could still blush, even after the things they had done together. She liked the idea that he could be a passionate lover, yet still be the same shy, sweet guy she had fallen for. "Do you want some coffee?" he asked, oblivious to her train of thought.

"Yes, I'd love some."

"Well, it might help if you'd let me go." Now it was her turn to blush. She released her grip on him and took a step backward. He took a mug out of a cabinet and filled it from the coffeepot that sat on the counter. "Milk or sugar?" he asked.

She couldn't believe he could act like he woke up with her in his bed every morning while she was reeling. "Lots of both," she said absently, admiring him as he opened the refrigerator to get the milk. On second thought, she decided she liked this normalcy. It was nice, being in his kitchen while he made her breakfast and prepared her a cup of coffee as if it were a prized delicacy. She could get used to this.

She thanked him for the mug of coffee he handed her, and she sipped at it while he took plates from the cabinet and arranged pancakes and bacon on them. "I'll let you put on your own butter and syrup," he said, setting the plates on the table. They each took seats at the table and began eating in silence.

Maddy ate until her stomach quit feeling empty. Despite his protestations of modesty about his cooking, he made decent pancakes. It took him a bit longer to take care of his hunger, and she watched him eat as she sipped at her coffee. Finally, she couldn't wait any longer. "Derek?" she asked. "Now what?"

"We could read the newspaper, and the Bugs Bunny show should be on soon. Or would you rather watch CNN?"

She couldn't help but smile as she shook her head. "That wasn't what I meant. I meant, where do we go from here?"

He studied her for a moment, and she could see the consideration he gave her question reflected in his steady blue eyes. "I think," he said slowly, "that this doesn't change much. Like you said last night, we're friends. I think we always will be, and that's good. I also know that I care about you." He glanced down at the table as a flush ran up his neck to his hairline, then he looked her in the eye. "And I love you. If I had my way, forever would be like this, waking up with you next to me, beginning my day with you and talking about everything and nothing over breakfast. Does that answer your question?"

She nodded. Then she smiled. "So I guess there's going to be more than three dates?"

"If you don't mind."

"Not at all. And, Derek, I want you to know that you're the most wonderful man I could possibly have found, with or without that silly book. I wish I'd been able to see you for what you were sooner."

"Maybe we weren't ready sooner."

"And you're even wise." She reached across the table to place her hand on his. "Actually, I must confess I used to have a big crush on you. Then it faded a bit, and then I got to know the real you and I fell in love, instead."

He answered her by leaning across the table to kiss her lips. She tasted the sweetness of syrup on his lips, as well as the sweetness of the promise his kiss held.

"There's just one problem," she said when they broke off the kiss.

"What's that?"

"How are we going to handle the last column? We're going to have to put our names on it this time, and everyone's going to figure out what happened, especially around the newsroom."

"They're going to figure it out, anyway. I don't intend to go sneaking around."

She sighed. "I suppose you're right. But how are we going to handle it?"

"Why don't we turn in a joint column from the two of us together and let people interpret it as they see fit?"

"You've got a computer here, don't you? Let's get to work."

### His and Hers

We must admit that we were both skeptical when we began this project. Love isn't something you can plan by some formula. It happens when you least expect it, and you find it in places you might never have looked. We also must confess that, in a way, the book worked. We each found someone special during the course of the assignment, but it wasn't exactly by following the tips in the book.

We didn't meet our special someone by going to nightclubs or supermarkets or walking a dog. We didn't meet at church or a political rally. We didn't meet in the mall, in a class or at an athletic event, and we didn't meet through mutual friends. But in a way, we did.

You see, we already knew each other—or, at least, we thought we did. But as we saw each other in each of these settings, we learned a little more about each other, and we realized that we had never looked beyond the surface. We liked the people we discovered underneath that surface.

We won't guarantee that following the steps in this book will work for everyone. In fact, we would almost say that doing these things will only work if you're not really looking for someone, but just going about your life.

Our advice? Go ahead and go to nightclubs and to grocery stores, walk your dog, visit the mall, take a class, join a church or an activist group and get to know your friends' friends. But don't do it because you want to meet someone. Do these things because they are things you want to do. Then, when you do these things, keep your eyes open. Also, take a good look at the people around you, those you see every day and those you've known for years. You never know who you'll discover.

And for those of you who haven't figured it out already, what we found on this assignment was each other.

Derek Newman and Madeline Hatfield

# *Epilogue*

#### ➤━━━◆

*Three months later*

From the *Dallas Journal:*

Coming up in Sunday's Life-style section, Derek Newman and Madeline Hatfield put another book to the test. This time they'll be checking out *The Ultimate Wedding Planner*. Read their weekly columns as they use this book to plan their own wedding. They'll be reporting on what works and what doesn't, and interpreting events in their own lively manner.

If you remember what happened the last time they tested a book, you won't want to miss a column.

Continuing in October from Silhouette Books...

This exciting new cross-line continuity series unites five of your favorite authors as they weave five connected novels about love, marriage—and Daddy's unexpected need for a baby carriage!

You loved

***THE BABY NOTION*** by Dixie Browning
(Desire 7/96)

***BABY IN A BASKET*** by Helen R. Myers
(Romance 8/96)

***MARRIED...WITH TWINS!*** by Jennifer Mikels
(Special Edition 9/96)

And the romance in New Hope, Texas, continues with:

***HOW TO HOOK A HUSBAND (AND A BABY)***
by Carolyn Zane (Yours Truly 10/96)

She vowed to get hitched by her thirtieth birthday. But plain-Jane Wendy Wilcox didn't have a clue how to catch herself a husband—until Travis, her sexy neighbor, offered to teach her what a man really wants in a wife....

And look for the thrilling conclusion to the series in:

***DISCOVERED: DADDY***
by Marilyn Pappano (Intimate Moments 11/96)

DADDY KNOWS LAST continues each month...
only in *Silhouette*®

# Take 4 bestselling love stories FREE

## Plus get a FREE surprise gift!

## Special Limited-time Offer

**Mail to Silhouette Reader Service™**

3010 Walden Avenue
P.O. Box 1867
Buffalo, N.Y. 14269-1867

**YES!** Please send me 4 free Silhouette Yours Truly™ novels and my free surprise gift. Then send me 4 brand-new novels every other month, which I will receive months before they appear in bookstores. Bill me at the low price of $2.69 each plus 25¢ delivery and applicable sales tax, if any.* That's the complete price and a savings of over 10% off the cover prices—quite a bargain! I understand that accepting the books and gift places me under no obligation ever to buy any books. I can always return a shipment and cancel at any time. Even if I never buy another book from Silhouette, the 4 free books and the surprise gift are mine to keep forever.

201 BPA AZH2

| | | |
|---|---|---|
| Name | (PLEASE PRINT) | |
| Address | Apt. No. | |
| City | State | Zip |

This offer is limited to one order per household and not valid to present Silhouette Yours Truly™ subscribers. *Terms and prices are subject to change without notice. Sales tax applicable in N.Y.

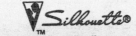

# As seen on TV!
## *Free Gift Offer*

With a Free Gift proof-of-purchase from any Silhouette® book, you can receive a beautiful cubic zirconia pendant.

This gorgeous marquise-shaped stone is a genuine cubic zirconia—accented by an 18" gold tone necklace.

(Approximate retail value $19.95)

## Send for yours today...

### compliments of ▼ *Silhouette*®

To receive your free gift, a cubic zirconia pendant, send us one original proof-of-purchase, photocopies not accepted, from the back of any Silhouette Romance™, Silhouette Desire®, Silhouette Special Edition®, Silhouette Intimate Moments® or Silhouette Yours Truly™ title available in August, September or October at your favorite retail outlet, together with the Free Gift Certificate, plus a check or money order for $1.65 U.S./$2.15 CAN. (do not send cash) to cover postage and handling, payable to Silhouette Free Gift Offer. We will send you the specified gift. Allow 6 to 8 weeks for delivery. Offer good until October 31, 1996 or while quantities last. Offer valid in the U.S. and Canada only.

## *Free Gift Certificate*

Name: _____

Address: _____

City: _____ State/Province: _____ Zip/Postal Code: _____

Mail this certificate, one proof-of-purchase and a check or money order for postage and handling to: SILHOUETTE FREE GIFT OFFER 1996. In the U.S.: 3010 Walden Avenue, P.O. Box 9077, Buffalo NY 14269-9077. In Canada: P.O. Box 613, Fort Erie, Ontario L2Z 5X3.

---

## FREE GIFT OFFER                                    084-KMD
ONE PROOF-OF-PURCHASE

To collect your fabulous FREE GIFT, a cubic zirconia pendant, you must include this original proof-of-purchase for each gift with the properly completed Free Gift Certificate.

---

**084-KMD**

## The Calhoun Saga continues...

in November
*New York Times* bestselling author

# NORA ROBERTS

takes us back to the Towers and introduces us to
the newest addition to the Calhoun household,
sister-in-law Megan O'Riley in

## MEGAN'S MATE
(Intimate Moments #745)

And in December
look in retail stores for the special collectors'
trade-size edition of

# THE
# Calhoun
# Women

containing all four fabulous Calhoun series books:
*COURTING CATHERINE,*
*A MAN FOR AMANDA, FOR THE LOVE OF LILAH*
and *SUZANNA'S SURRENDER.*
Available wherever books are sold.

## Bestselling Author
# BARBARA BOSWELL

Continues the twelve-book series—FORTUNE'S CHILDREN—
in **October 1996** with Book Four

## STAND-IN BRIDE

When Fortune Company executive Michael Fortune needed help
warding off female admirers after being named one of the ten most
eligible bachelors in the United States, he turned to his faithful
assistant, Julia Chandler. Julia agreed to a pretend engagement, but
what starts as a charade produces an unexpected Fortune heir....

MEET THE FORTUNES—a family whose legacy is greater than riches.
Because where there's a will...there's a *wedding!*

"Ms. Boswell is one of those rare treasures who combines humor
and romance into sheer magic." —*Rave Reviews*

*A CASTING CALL TO*
*ALL FORTUNE'S CHILDREN FANS!*
If you are truly one of the fortunate
you may win a trip to
Los Angeles to audition for
Wheel of Fortune®. Look for
details in all retail Fortune's Children titles!

Look us up on-line at: http://www.romance.net

FC-4-C

# 1997
## Reader's Engagement Book
## A calendar of important dates
## and anniversaries for readers to use!

Informative and entertaining—with notable
dates and trivia highlighted throughout the year.

Handy, convenient, pocketbook size to help you
keep track of your own personal important dates.

Added bonus—contains $5.00 worth of coupons
for upcoming Harlequin and Silhouette books.
This calendar more than pays for itself!

 Available beginning in November at
your favorite retail outlet.

 HARLEQUIN®

# You're About to Become a

*Privileged Woman*

Reap the rewards of fabulous free gifts and benefits with proofs-of-purchase from Silhouette and Harlequin books

# Pages & Privileges™

It's our way of thanking you for buying our books at your favorite retail stores.

**PROOF OF PURCHASE**

YT-PP186

Offer expires October 31, 1996

Pages & Privileges ™

Harlequin and Silhouette—
the most privileged readers in the world!

For more information about Harlequin and Silhouette's PAGES & PRIVILEGES program call the Pages & Privileges Benefits Desk: 1-503-794-2499

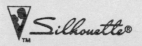

*Silhouette*®

TM